## "I hope you don't mind my calling you at work, Jacob."

Liza's voice actually sounded shy, if that could be believed, thought Jake.

"Oh, I don't mind at all." He was proud of how incredibly casual he sounded.

"I was wondering if..." Liza hesitated.

"If what?"

"Do you think we could get together when you have some time?"

"I suppose that could be arranged." How cool his reply was, he congratulated himself.

"It's just that..." Liza was suddenly at a loss for words. After all, she reasoned, how did one arrange a meeting to tell a man you might be in love with him? With all her vast knowledge of etiquette and experience in protocol, this was one predicament in which she showed an appalling lack of expertise.

"It's just *what*, Liza?" It was obvious she'd had second thoughts about her behavior last night and now wanted to offer the traditional olive branch. Fine. He would show her just how forgiving and magnanimous he could be—even with her.

"Oh, I'll tell you when I see you," Liza said, suddenly shy all over again.

Dear Reader:

The spirit of the Silhouette Romance Homecoming Celebration lives on as each month we bring you six books by continuing stars!

And there are some wonderful stories in the stars for you. In the coming months, we're publishing romances by many of your favorite authors such as Sondra Stanford, Annette Broadrick and Brittany Young. In addition, we have some very special events planned for the summer of 1988.

In June, watch for the first book in Diana Palmer's exciting new trilogy, Long, Tall Texans. The initial title, *Calhoun*, will be followed later by *Justin* and *Tyler*. All three books are designed to capture your heart.

Also in June is Phyllis Halldorson's *Raindance Autumn*, the second book of this wonderful author's Raindance Duo. Don't miss this exciting sequel!

Your response to these authors and other authors of Silhouette Romances has served as a touchstone for us, and we're pleased to bring you more books with Silhouette's distinctive medley of charm, wit and—above all—*romance*.

I hope you enjoy this book and the many stories to come. Come home to Silhouette—for always!

Sincerely,

Tara Hughes
Senior Editor
Silhouette Books

# VICTORIA GLENN

# Moon in the Water

*Silhouette Romance*

Published by Silhouette Books New York

**America's Publisher of Contemporary Romance**

To my wonderfully patient editor,
Tara Hughes,
who understands the importance of deadlines,
dessert and Disneyland

SILHOUETTE BOOKS
300 E. 42nd St., New York, N.Y. 10017

Copyright © 1988 by Victoria Dann

ISBN: 0-373-08585-0

First Silhouette Books printing June 1988

---

## VICTORIA GLENN,

an award-winning writer herself, comes from a family of writers. She makes her home in the Connecticut countryside but divides her time between the East and West Coasts. She considers it essential to the creative process to visit Disneyland at least twice a year.

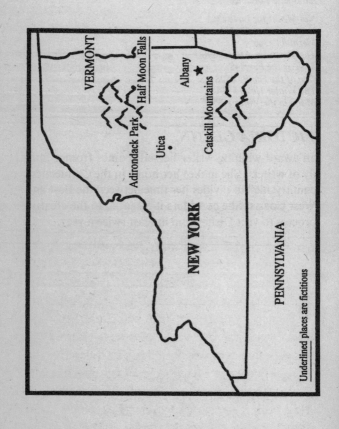

VERMONT

Half Moon Falls

Albany ★

Adirondack Park

Catskill Mountains

Utica

NEW YORK

PENNSYLVANIA

Underlined places are fictitious

# *Chapter One*

As the only daughter of celebrated statesman Ambassador Arthur Langley, Elizabeth Langley had grown up in an aura of wealth and privilege. In the normal course of affairs, Liza might never have met Tracy MacBride. To say that the two of them moved in different social circles would have been an understatement. Nevertheless, Liza and Tracy had been best friends for five years, ever since sharing the same freshman composition class in college. In the time they'd known each other, Liza remembered, Tracy seldom spoke of her home in the mountains of New York State, except to say, "I suppose I come from the wrong side of the tracks—only Half Moon Falls doesn't even have a railroad."

"Or much of anything else," Liza now murmured as she pulled her car into the town's only gas station. Well, one couldn't really call Half Moon Falls a town. It looked more like a sleepy little village. Looking around her, she decided she must have entered a time warp. It was six-thirty in the morning and the sun was barely beginning its ascent into the sky. The pretty frame houses, all of which seemed to have picket fences, dotted the shadowy green landscape like little white toys. On a small hill, overseeing it all, was an old country church with a tall steeple. The entire impression was of something right out of a storybook.

Liza gave a weary yawn. Perhaps this place only appeared half-real because she was still half-asleep. She had been driving all night, after all, a practice she didn't really approve of. But in this particular situation the need to put all current stress behind her had spurred an urgency of action.

It had been a dreadful, disastrous week. Even as a self-assured young woman who had spent most of her life in the public eye, Liza had found the events of the past few days too much to handle. So she had fled Washington, D.C., to escape the low whispers, the curious looks and the glare of the cameras. She had never felt so alone, so isolated, in her entire life. And the only person who could possibly understand was Tracy. She could almost hear her saying, "Heck, Liz! What are friends for?"

Good old Tracy. It had been months since they had last spoken to each other. The truth was, Liza hadn't had much time for anything or anyone else during her engagement to Mark. But she knew that it didn't matter to Tracy, because good friends have a shorthand all their own. It never seemed to matter how long the interval between their last conversation had been. They were always ready to pick up exactly where they left off. Liza sighed as she scanned the horizon. Yes, coming to this remote little hamlet had been a sensible decision. Even though her visit was somewhat out of the blue, she was sure Tracy would be delighted to see her.

She glanced around impatiently for a service attendant, then, finally noticing the darkened windows of the small building, realized the place obviously was still closed. Great, just great! Liza had been hoping to find someone who could give her directions to Tracy's house. If only she could call her friend, but there wasn't a phone booth in sight. All Liza had with her was a makeshift map sent by Tracy long ago. The problem was that none of these country lanes seemed to have any signs.

Starting up the engine again, Liza turned out of the deserted parking area. The quiet rural highway was equally deserted. Driving by the numerous old houses, she was unable to detect a single light from within. The place seemed dead to the world. She wondered how bright, bubbly Tracy could stand to be buried in this tiny hamlet in the middle of nowhere. What did people do for fun around here? Where did they go on a Saturday night? Liza gave a short laugh. Well, hadn't she wanted to get away from it all? From the looks of this place she had gotten away from just about *everything*.

Suddenly her thoughts were pierced by the blast of a car horn and the screech of tires. Only then did Liza notice the sharp curve and a pickup truck careening wildly toward her. An icy stab of horror scarcely had time to penetrate before she desperately steered away from the oncoming vehicle and stomped her brakes to the floor.

The vintage Mustang skidded off the road and bounced to an abrupt stop on the rocky shoulder. With a sigh of relief Liza buried her face against the leather-covered steering wheel. Her heart was racing wildly, and her mouth was bitter with the sickly taste that accompanied a brush with death.

Then she remembered the other driver. Oh, God! What had happened to the people in the truck? She flung open the door and stumbled toward the dusty blue pickup. It was all in one piece, Liza noted with relief, and had come to a rest on the grassy slope along the other side of the road.

Just then a man emerged from the cab. Three things registered instantly. He was tall. He was ugly. He was mad. Blazing mad.

"Who the hell gave you a license, lady?" The black, angry words almost spat out of his mouth.

"You could have gotten us both killed! Of all the stupid, idiotic..."

Liza absorbed his violent tirade, struck momentarily dumb. Never in her life had she been the object of such rage. Men, in particular, did not speak to Elizabeth Langley like this. It simply wasn't done.

"And if you read the road signs, that is *presuming* you can read, you would have known that this is a blind curve...."

She continued to listen to his ravings with a mixture of shock and fascination. It was somewhat refreshing to be treated like anybody else. Liza had the instant impression that this was a man who deferred to no one. And at that moment she revised her previous assessment of him. He wasn't ugly. Just big and mad. Everything about him was dark—his hair, his eyes, even the expression on his hard, tanned face. He wore a black nylon windbreaker and matching dungarees. And there was something indescribably virile about him.

"You haven't heard a word I've said, have you, lady?" he barked.

Liza drew herself up to her full height of five feet, four inches. Refreshing had its limits, after all. Enough was enough. "Not only are you rude, but you are also wrong," she began coldly. "I was in my lane. You swerved out of yours. Kindly reserve your misplaced macho indignation for the local females who might be gullible enough to interpret your crude bellowings as rustic charm."

The man's mouth practically dropped open, Liza noted with a degree of satisfaction. His strange dark eyes narrowed. "So," he uttered slowly, "it talks."

Liza bristled. "Oh, I talk. However, I think first, which is more than I can say for you."

His lips compressed into a thin smile. "Sharp little thing, aren't you?"

The nerve of this hayseed, using that superior tone with her! "Judging from your rather limited vocabulary, it's obvious that English is your second language. What's your native tongue—Early Neanderthal?"

The man didn't say anything for a moment, he simply stared at her with raised eyebrows. It was evident that he wasn't used to being spoken to in such a manner by a mere *woman*. He seemed to look at Liza for the first time, appraising her slowly, from the long, disheveled blond hair tumbling out of its restraining barrette to her blue-gray eyes, no doubt bright with indignation, to her skin, pale and clear without benefit of makeup, although she could feel the flush beginning to tint her cheeks. His frank gaze roamed lower, pausing at the soft curves of her breasts, braless beneath the oversize sweatshirt.

"Someone ought to teach you a lesson," he murmured under his breath.

"Oh, I'm *really* scared," Liza retorted, crossing her arms. The situation was intimidating, but she recognized the importance of not showing fear. Instinctively she knew the man would not hurt her.

His mouth twisted. "I bet underneath all that acid and chicken wire beats the heart of a frustrated young woman. That is," he paused, "assuming you have a heart."

"Probably not," Liza replied glibly. Two could play this game. Nobody had ever been able to bait *her*.

"Well, well. A woman talks like that and it can only mean one thing...."

"How original. According to conceited males such as yourself, it always means one so-called *thing*."

A sudden, amused smile unexpectedly softened his features. "And what thing is that, honey?"

Who was he to call her "honey"? Liza felt a tiny bubble of outrage growing larger and larger. She hadn't had much time for anger during this past week. More than anything else her reaction to Mark's betrayal had been shock, surprise and then an odd numbness. It was as if now, at long last, she was ready to release the fury that had been bottled up inside. Why else would she even be standing here in the middle of nowhere, arguing with this arrogant stranger? This overbearing, chauvinistic bumpkin?

"What's the matter?" came the silky taunt. "Cat got your tongue?"

"Listen Clem—or Hiram or Homer or whatever your name is—this strutting-rooster routine might work fine at the Saturday-night barn dance, but to me you're just the farmer in the dell. So why don't you head on back to that rusty hunk of junk you've been driving and be thankful you haven't done any real damage!'' This flow of invective astonished even herself. Liza was usually in perfect control of her emotions. But no man had ever made her feel so *provoked*.

His jaw tightened perceptibly, but he didn't answer.

"What's the matter," she mimicked, "cat got your tongue?"

Slowly, deliberately, the man raised his head. "No," came the cool reply. "More like a kitten. A kitten with claws."

Liza had been trained at an early age to recognize a potentially dangerous situation and remove herself from the source of danger as quickly and discreetly as possible. But this morning her reaction time was off. Maybe it had to do with the fact that she was tired from the long drive. What other explanation could there be?

But suddenly the expression on the man's face changed. "Is your car all right?" he asked in a different voice.

"Yes, no thanks to you," she shot back, relieved that the emphasis of the confrontation had shifted to something safe and inanimate.

"If you were at all familiar with these roads," he rebuked, "you wouldn't be so hasty to shift the burden of blame to the other driver. As it so happens, I had the right of way."

"And you're never wrong," Liza observed.

"Obviously you aren't from around here."

"A state of affairs that pleases me no end," she murmured half-aloud. What strange power was holding her here, anyhow? Why was she unable to move away from this disturbing encounter and return to the peace and security of her own car?

"What brings you to our tranquil community, city girl?" he probed.

"As if it's any of your business," Liza muttered. This was all rather bewildering. She hadn't even known this creature for five minutes, and already he was the most irritating human being she had ever met.

"Everything that goes on in Half Moon Falls is my business."

"What an exciting life you must lead!"

"I have the feeling you aren't taking me very seriously, young lady." The velvet tone belied a warning edge of steel beneath the surface.

"Does anybody?" Liza was proceeding carelessly, but what did it matter? It had been ages since she'd had this much fun.

The man in black inhaled sharply. "Does anybody *what*?"

"Take you seriously."

"Keep provoking me like this, honey, and I won't be responsible for my actions." It was a thinly veiled threat.

*I must be losing my mind,* Liza said to herself. *I'm alone on a mountain road at six in the morning car-*

*rying on a ludicrous conversation with a sexist yo-
kel!*

But to her adversary she merely shrugged. "Since
neither of our vehicles appears to have sustained any
damage, we have nothing further to discuss."

"Just a minute—"

Liza ignored this harsh command. "It's been a
thrill meeting you," she saluted casually over her
shoulder and returned to her waiting Mustang.

The man did not reply. He merely stood there,
rooted to the spot. He still wasn't moving a muscle
when Liza slid into the driver's seat and checked the
rearview mirror. He just continued to stare. Hastily
Liza turned the key in the ignition and put the car
into gear. Pulling back onto the country highway, she
glanced into the mirror once more as she drove off.
The figure in black grew smaller and smaller in the
distance. Liza gave a sigh of relief.

She sincerely hoped she would never run into *that*
person again. One such encounter was more than
enough. It occurred to her that under any other circumstances she might have asked him for directions
to Tracy's house. He seemed to know everything and
everybody around here, if, indeed, he had spoken the
truth. On the other hand, Liza couldn't very well
have placed herself in the awkward position of asking *that* man's assistance for anything. She didn't
need to subject herself to his superior attitude by
asking him for a favor.

What was it about men? Whether they were politicians, like Mark, or farmers, as this one obviously was, they were all insufferable. Although there was something especially annoying about this one—an indefinable "something" Liza had never come up against before. An unknown quality.

He was just a man, she chided herself hastily. And an ill-bred one at that. She would waste no further energy thinking about him. The very purpose of this impromptu trip was to get away from just such a source of masculine aggravation. Men were nothing but trouble. She'd often watched the absurdities of high-level diplomacy and decided that if women ran the world, it would be a much better place.

The road continued to dip and wind through rolling hills. Liza flipped down the visor as the sun began to stream through the windshield. Suddenly, once again out of nowhere, there appeared another vehicle. This time it was a young boy on a shiny new bicycle, the wire rear baskets stacked with newspapers. Probably the *Half Moon Falls Gazette*, Liza thought wryly. She waved to the rider and brought the car to a stop. He was blond and chubby, with the obligatory smattering of freckles. He stared at her curiously, his arms hunched up against the handlebars.

"Would you happen to know where Meadowview Lane is?"

He shrugged. "You're on it, lady."

"By any chance, do you know the MacBrides?"

"Sure, Gary and Tommy are in my class."

Liza remembered the names. They were Tracy's little brothers.

"That's their house," the youngster said, pointing to a tiny red structure in the distance, "across the hill." He examined the red convertible admiringly. "Nice car!" He waved to her and pedaled off.

Well, thought Liza. Not every male around here was as insufferable as that character in the black windbreaker. Just thinking about him gave her an involuntary shudder. But the thought was pushed from her mind as she finally approached the old-fashioned metal mailbox with a red flag perched on top and MacBride painted on the side in letters four inches high.

Beyond the mailbox was an attractive farmhouse, trimmed in white, with an aging porch and railing winding around all sides. Several trucks and cars in various stages of disrepair were parked unceremoniously on a large patch of overgrown grass. An unmistakable aroma wafted to Liza's nostrils. Freshly baked bread. At least she wouldn't be waking anybody up, she thought with relief. Moments later she knocked on the front door, which seemed sadly in need of a fresh paint job.

An astonished figure in cotton pajamas flung open the screen door. "Liz!" she screeched happily. "I can't believe it!"

"Tracy," Liza said, smiling back at her old friend. "I was in the neighborhood, so I thought I'd drop in."

"Is that all you can say?" Tracy shook her head in disbelief.

"How about 'you're certainly up with the chickens'?"

As Tracy led her into the house Liza noted she hadn't changed a bit. Still skinny as a rail, with that short mop of unruly red hair and the broadest grin she could remember. It was so good to see her friend again. The family tragedy that had forced Tracy MacBride to interrupt her education and return to this obscure country town to care for her twin brothers didn't appear to have sapped any vitality from her spirited face.

"I just can't believe you're here!" she repeated.

"I'm here, all right." Liza stood in the small kitchen and gazed at the rows of loaf pans cooling along the ceramic countertop.

Tracy followed her stare. "I couldn't sleep. I decided to do a little baking."

"A *little*?"

"I guess I'll freeze some and use it for the boys' sandwiches or something." She paused. "I heard about you and Mark."

"Does the whole world know?" Liza was incredulous.

"Come on, Liz. Mark Sheridan is a U.S. senator!"

Liza shrugged. "This isn't Washington."

"Okay, so maybe I didn't exactly read about it in the *Half Moon Falls Gazette*—"

"Thank goodness," Liza groaned, "that would be all I need!"

"I read about it in *World People Magazine*."

Liza cleared her throat quickly. "Uh, why don't we have some coffee."

Tracy grinned understandingly. "Okay, but I want to hear everything. All the gossip."

It was pleasant to sit in the haphazardly furnished little living room, sipping coffee and munching on delicious white bread, hot from the oven. The two of them had so much to catch up on. When they had attended American University, in Washington, D.C., Tracy had found it difficult to make ends meet, even with her scholarship. But she had her pride, which made it almost impossible for Liza to do anything for her—which was frustrating since there was a great deal she might have done for her best friend, considering that the Langley family fortune was one of the largest in the country.

Tracy had steadfastly refused monetary help whenever Liza had offered it, and when Tracy stood firm on a matter, she simply wouldn't budge. Take for example the horrible circumstances that had forced her to withdraw from the university halfway through graduate school.

Tracy's aunt and uncle had been killed in a car accident, and there'd been no one left to take care of the twins, who were ten years old. She'd never spoken much about her own parents, and Liza acknowledged that it was a sensitive subject. The longer she knew Tracy, the more convinced she became that there was more to the situation than met the eye. But she also realized that it was useless to force the issue. One day, Liza believed, her friend would finally open up to her and explain whatever dark secret haunted the MacBride family closet.

In any event, Tracy had packed up and left Washington four months ago. It didn't matter that she was now walking away from everything she had struggled to achieve. It didn't even matter that she despised the country town where she had grown up and had sworn never to return there. All that mattered to Tracy MacBride was that her family needed her, and blood was thicker than water.

"So," Tracy said now, replenishing their empty coffee mugs, "You're not going to marry Mark, after all."

Liza had known her friend long enough to detect something else in her tone. "You don't sound very surprised."

There was an awkward pause. "Another fairy tale bites the dust."

Liza could scarcely believe the cynical tone in her voice. Could this possibly be Tracy, the most lighthearted creature she had ever known? "And here I thought you were the one person left on earth who still believed in fairy tales."

"I do, sometimes."

"Then why do I get the distinct impression that you aren't telling me something?"

Tracy sighed. "I really didn't know how to tell you before. I mean, you're my dearest friend and everything." She stopped.

"Would you tell me already?" Liza shot back impatiently.

"Well, it's just that I promised myself if you ever went through with it and actually married the guy, I wouldn't ever tell you."

"Wouldn't tell me *what*?"

Tracy set down her mug uncomfortably. "Liz, before I moved back here that hotshot fiancé of yours made a pass at me."

"I see." A flush of mortification coursed through her. She was mad at Mark and mad at herself for having been so blind. Liza only wished her best friend had told her all this before, yet she understood Tracy's predicament.

"Are you angry at me?"

"No." How could anyone ever be angry with Tracy? As if it were even her fault. In the past week, a clearer picture of Mark had begun to coalesce in her mind. Since their engagement a year ago the concept of unfaithfulness had never crossed her mind as a remote possibility. Mark Sheridan and Elizabeth Langley had been a stunning couple, an appropriate couple. The junior senator from the Midwest had seemed a dream come true. Tender yet forceful, handsome yet unpretentious, he was just as much at home in the White House as he was at a fast-food restaurant. And best of all, he was part of the world she had grown up in.

Theirs had been a union that even the ultracritical Arthur Langley had endorsed wholeheartedly. He'd informed his daughter the engagement was a perfect match, and Liza, who had been waiting twenty-three years for perfection, had been swept along with the fantasy. And that's all it had been, she acknowledged now with a trace of bitterness. Just a fantasy. The discovery of Mark's string of affairs with a succession of pretty young women had ended everything. There would be no happily-ever-after.

"You look angry," Tracy said in a small voice, still waiting to be reassured.

"I'm angry at myself."

"At yourself? I don't understand."

*For believing in Prince Charming and knights in shining armor,* Liza chastised herself silently.

"Liz?" Tracy repeated with concern.

Liza gave a tired smile. "Oh, never mind. It doesn't matter now. So—" she glanced around the brightening room as more sunlight began flooding in through the paned windows "—what are your plans for the rest of the day?"

Tracy stretched her lanky legs across the threadbare sofa and yawned. "It's Saturday. Who has any plans for Saturday?"

Saturday! That must be why she'd seen hardly a soul in town. Liza shook her head deprecatingly. What had happened to her mind in this past week? No doubt about it, she needed a rest. A long, peaceful rest.

"Of course," Tracy chattered away, "when the twins finally drag themselves out of bed, they'll be so excited to meet you."

"Told them about me, huh?"

An odd expression came over Tracy. "Actually, they only know that there's a wonderful girl named Liz, who's their big sister's best pal. You see, I—" She hesitated again. "It's like this. I grew up here, in a town where practically everybody knows everybody else. There's no such thing as a secret, almost. Getting that scholarship and going away to school was the first time in my life I ever had any privacy. And for five years I've kept it that way...." She shrugged. "That is, until I moved back here again." The suspicion of a tear welled in her eye. "God, Liz. I wish I—" Tracy stopped, and a tone of artificial brightness colored her voice. "Hey, I bet you're really tired, huh?"

"Tracy." Liza couldn't be fooled. "When are you going to tell me what's wrong?"

"Nothing's wrong." Her friend's voice was just a bit too high-pitched.

Liza knew one of the things that had kept the two of them friends for the past five years was that both knew when not to push an issue. When Tracy was ready to confide in her, she would. Right now, Liza decided, it was best to drop the subject.

"Let me show you your room," Tracy was saying quite cheerfully now. "It isn't much, but at least the roof doesn't leak." She led the way up the rickety wooden staircase to a sloped attic room with faded flowered wallpaper, several mismatched pieces of furniture and an attractive double bed with an oak headboard. A full-length oval mirror stood in the corner, and a collection of photographs in old frames cluttered the dresser top.

"This used to be my room," Tracy explained suddenly. "My aunt and uncle set it up for me when I first came to live with them."

"It's very pretty."

"Yeah, well, I moved into the master bedroom after I came back this time. It's easier keeping an eye on the boys if I'm downstairs." Tracy paused and glanced around the attic room wistfully. "I miss it up here sometimes, though."

Suddenly there was a loud crash, like a chair falling over, followed by the high-pitched shouts of two young voices. Tracy rolled her eyes. "Speaking of the devil. I do believe the little monsters have awakened." She headed for the landing, and Liza could hear more shouting and doors slamming from below. "Hey, you guys," Tracy boomed over the railing, "I'm giving you to the count of three to pipe down or you're in big trouble!" She turned her head toward Liza and sighed. "I'd better go down alone.

I don't think you're quite ready to charge into the jungle yet. Let me get Jekyll and Hyde subdued before introducing them to company." She charged down the stairs, leaving Liza alone in the attic room.

Rubbing her eyes with fatigue, Liza wandered over to the tall heavy dresser and began to unpack her nylon carryall. Idly she inspected the cluster of photos that appeared to have been taken during Tracy's time in high school. Tracy in a cheerleading costume, smiling up at a gangly boy in a football uniform. Tracy in what was obviously a prom setting, arm in arm with the same boy, who now wore an ill-fitting white tuxedo. There was something disturbingly familiar about the boy, and then Liza remembered why. He bore an uncanny resemblance to the angry man in the pickup truck. But the boy in these pictures couldn't have been more than seventeen or eighteen, while the man she had met this morning appeared to have been somewhere in his late thirties. Liza was unusually curious to discover what, if anything, was the connection. Brothers, perhaps? Or cousins? It certainly was a small enough town for such a practical explanation.

And then she remembered something else—what that disturbing man had said to her as they stood across from each other on a lonely country road: "Everything that goes on in Half Moon Falls is my business."

Liza felt an inexplicable tingle down the back of her neck. She saw her best friend's life exposed to the scrutiny of the man in the black jacket. There were no secrets in Half Moon Falls, Tracy had told her. And this man knew everything. But what kind of *everything* were they talking about? Liza recalled the whispered confidences and earth-shattering slices of information that floated discreetly through the rare-fied air of high diplomatic circles. Because of who she was, there had been many secrets that Liza had inadvertently become privy to over the years. So how awesome could the secrets of Tracy MacBride and Half Moon Falls be when compared to the chilling compendium of international skeletons hiding in the well-locked closets of the most powerful govern-ments in the world?

For heaven's sake, this wasn't Washington, D.C., the nation's capital. It was only Half Moon Falls, New York, a mere rustic hole-in-the-wall.

And then she looked at the prom photograph again, and a strange chill came over Liza when she gazed into the face of Tracy's escort.

# Chapter Two

Either Gary or Tommy MacBride alone would have been a handful, but together they comprised the naughtiest, yet most delightful, ten-year-old duo Liza had ever seen. A more mischievous set of twins she had never encountered. Physically they resembled scaled-down versions of Tracy, with the same wild red hair and impudent grin. The two of them were so much a part of each other that it was difficult to determine where one ended and the other began. They always seemed to be whispering and plotting, conspiring new ways to wreak havoc on their long-suffering school teachers and bus drivers. But they adored their older sister and instantly took a liking to Liza, which she deemed extremely fortunate.

"You're pretty," they said in unison when Tracy introduced them after breakfast.

"She also plays baseball," Tracy added meaningfully with a wink at her friend.

"Would you play with us?" the twins asked eagerly.

Liza smiled, instantly enamored with both of them. "Sure."

"No, you guys," Tracy interrupted firmly. "Liz is going to rest first. She's been driving all night."

"She makes you take naps, too?" they asked Liza in disbelief.

Liza exchanged amused glances with Tracy. "She's bossy, all right."

"But not as bossy as Uncle Jake," declared Tommy.

"Who's he?" Liza asked Tracy.

Tracy shifted in her seat uneasily and cleared her throat. "I want to be alone with Liz, so go outside and play."

"We don't wanna," protested the twins. "We wanna stay here and talk to Liz, too."

"I said beat it, you guys, or it's liver for dinner." The boys made identical expressions of disgust and, without further protest, dashed out of the house.

"You certainly know how to handle them," Liza observed.

"I love them to pieces, but sometimes they drive me nuts," Tracy confessed, sitting down on a cushion. She hesitated.

Liza crossed her arms. "Okay, you want to tell me about it now?"

"I feel kind of funny about this. I mean, you've come up here to get away from your own problems, not be snowed under with mine." Tracy stared out the window at her brothers playing on a tire swing in the yard.

Actually Liza *wanted* to be snowed under with another person's problems. What better way to forget her own? In the past year Liza had been so occupied with her role as the future wife of an up-and-coming political star that she'd been—it was shameful to admit—blind to the turmoil in her best friend's life. She was eager to make up for it now. "Talk to me, Trace."

There was an uncomfortable pause, and then her friend burst out, "I hate this place. I've always hated it. But if I hadn't come back when I did, I would have lost Tommy and Gary."

"What do you mean, you would have lost them?"

"He would have taken them away from me."

"Who?"

"Jacob." Tracy took a deep breath. "Jacob Van Cleef."

"Wait a minute." Liza paused thoughtfully. "Are you talking about the person they call Uncle Jake?"

Tracy nodded. "Only he isn't their uncle."

"So what's the problem? You're their sister, and you're over twenty-one. Nobody can take the boys away from you."

"*He* can."

Liza was baffled. "Trace, as far as I can tell, if the man isn't even a relative, he doesn't have a leg to stand on."

"He owns this town, Liz. He can do anything he wants."

Liza lowered her legs to the floor and settled down next to her troubled companion. "Putting aside the fact that this is America and we're not in the Dark Ages, would you kindly explain why this Mr. Van Cleef wants to take the twins away from you?"

"Because—" Tracy stifled a sob "—he says they need a father or they'll become juvenile delinquents."

"I've never heard of such a thing!" Liza fumed.

"He can do it, Liz." Tracy's eyes began to well up again. "He can take my brothers away from me."

Liza placed an arm around her. "Nonsense, he can't do anything of the kind." But she was still bothered by a disturbing thought: why would a man want to take two young children away from a loving relative? Something didn't sit right.

"He hates me, Liz. His entire family hates me."

Hate Tracy? The very idea was absurd. Who in the world could hate Tracy? Even the fastidious Arthur Langley, who had never concealed his impatience for most of his daughter's friends, had always been fond of Tracy. There had never been a time when Tracy had not been welcome in the Langley home. The thought of anyone bearing ill will toward her gentle friend riled Liza, but she tried to temper her reaction.

"Trace, I can't believe that the Van Cleefs *hate* you."

"Trust me," Tracy said bitterly, "they hate me."

Liza sighed. "Why?"

"I'm from the wrong side of the tracks, remember?"

"People don't think that way anymore. It's the twentieth century."

Tracy wasn't convinced. "Maybe in the rest of the country; but here it's still the nineteenth century. We're pretty provincial."

"Trace," Liza said, scratching her head skeptically. "I consider myself quite an authority on the class system—" Well, it was true. After all, the Langley name had been synonymous with American royalty for generations.

Tracy guffawed. "Do you think being Elizabeth Langley makes you an authority on snobbery? So you've acted as hostess at diplomatic soirees that would make most people's heads spin. So that British prince what's-his-name came to your sweet sixteen party. And who could forget the time you got the president's wife to take our American history class on a private tour of the White House—"

"Please, don't rub it in!" Liza interrupted. For some reason, her friend's words embarrassed her.

"The point is, Liz, that you come from a social level so high up you've been flying above the weather. The real snobs don't come from your kind of elite but from a few rungs lower."

Liza could understand what her friend was trying to say. During her years at boarding school she'd often been amused by the airs put on by girls whose families were neither as wealthy or important as many of the others. She realized it was believable that in the closed social system of a country town a person could be locked into a particular role for life.

"They say I'm too young to raise two kids on my own." Tracy continued to stare out the window dejectedly.

"Who are 'they'?"

"Not just the Van Cleefs but everybody in this town."

"Don't people around here have anything better to do than mind your business?" Liza decided one could easily go bananas in Half Moon Falls.

"You don't understand, Liz." Tracy sighed. "There's something—" She stopped. "Oh, heck. I don't want to talk about this anymore. I just get too upset."

"Trace—"

"No, Liz. I feel funny telling you this much." She glanced at her watch. "Look, I promised the boys I'd drive them over to Silverwood Lake to visit their friends, and I know it would bore you to distraction. Besides, you look tired enough to drop."

Tracy was right, Liza thought. The drowsiness was certainly starting to hit. So she didn't protest her friend's suggestion that she catch up on some sleep for the rest of the day while Tracy played chauffeur. They made plans to have a wonderful dinner in the late afternoon when Tracy and the twins returned.

After the three MacBrides had left, Liza trudged wearily up to her room and promptly fell asleep, fully clothed. It was only two o'clock when she awoke, fully refreshed, and took a brief shower. As the warm water sprayed away the last traces of dust and grime, she decided that this little unplanned vacation was just what the doctor had ordered. After all, when was the last time her life had been truly her own?

When Liza's mother had died, Liza had been expected to continue the tradition as the perfect hostess. And so the very proper young lady, who had been educated at the best finishing schools money could buy, entertained with a style and grace seldom seen in women twice her age. A true diplomat's daughter, she was adept at smoothing the ruffled feathers of feuding ambassadors, keeping the dinner conversation lively and interesting and making any guest feel at ease. In many ways it was a full-time job. Unfortunately, no one ever bothered to ask Liza if there was something else she'd rather be doing.

Perhaps that was why she'd been considered a valuable asset to Senator Mark Sheridan's skyrocketing political aspirations...a stepping-stone to his career. A poised and well-groomed wife who didn't ask too many questions. Sure, it didn't hurt that Liza was pretty, but then what young woman with her wealth and connections wouldn't be? One year ago, as soon as their engagement had become official, Mark had insisted, very sweetly, of course, that Liza act as hostess for him, too. Only now did it occur to her that she hadn't particularly enjoyed it. Perhaps even back then, Liza now realized, she'd been cleverly manipulated and used.

She twisted her lips tightly and continued to brush out her long, blond hair. Freshly washed, it bounced over her shoulders in shiny waves. Tightening the sash around Tracy's short white cotton robe, Liza decided to go down to the kitchen for a thick slice of home-baked bread and butter. She couldn't help thinking about her friend and the heavy burden she must be carrying. At least she'd been able to make Tracy smile when she insisted her friend take the red Mustang up to the lake so they could all enjoy the open convertible. The twins had squealed with delight, and Tracy had sighed gratefully, explaining that the expensive German tape deck was sure to drown out the shrieks and yells of two boisterous ten-year-olds during the long drive.

Liza was just carrying a lavishly buttered hunk of bread on an earthenware plate into the living room when she heard a knock at the door. Balancing the dish in one hand, she threw open the front door with the other. "Back so soon—" she began, then stopped, frozen. Standing there with an equally astonished expression on his hard face was the man from this morning.

"You," he finally murmured in surprise and continued to stare at her wordlessly. There was something so penetrating in his gaze, so thorough about his appraisal that Liza felt as if she were half undressed—and then realized she was. The robe was almost indecently short to be wearing in front of strangers, and she remembered she was naked underneath the loosely tied sash and gaping terrycloth lapels. Nervously Liza gathered the front more closely around her slim body.

"I didn't expect to see you again," the man finally said. "You took off rather abruptly."

Liza flushed involuntarily. How could this be happening? She knew all the clever expressions about what a small world it could be, but this was ridiculous!

The dark, piercing eyes remained intently on her face. "I see that once again you're at a loss for words." He paused. "I assume you must be a friend of Tracy MacBride's."

"How astute. You must be a brain surgeon!" The sharp words flowed from her lips before Liza could stop them.

"Still as demure as I recall," the man retorted. "Suddenly I'm not very surprised that you're a buddy of Tracy's."

"And what is that supposed to mean?" Liza inquired icily.

"Of course!" he said, more to himself than to Liza. "It should have occurred to me when I saw that

District of Columbia license plate. You must be her friend from the university.''

She eyed him warily. ''How do you know that?''

''Didn't I tell you I know everything that goes on in Half Moon Falls?'' He gave a tight smile. ''Oh, I know a little about you.''

Liza shifted on her feet uncomfortably. ''Such as?''

''Your name is Liza, you've been friends since freshman year, and you and Tracy have hitchhiked through Europe during several summer breaks.''

''We *what*?'' Liza was incredulous.

''Take it from me,'' the man said coldly, showing his disapproval, ''it's a pretty brainless thing to do. Young girls just don't think . . .''

*Hitchhiked through Europe?* Is that how Tracy had explained away the times Liza had successfully convinced her to accompany the Langleys on their numerous trips to some of the most elegant places in the world? She'd begged, pleaded and finally coerced Tracy into coming along by convincing her friend that it wasn't charity. The hotel suite or villa in question always had tons of room, and her father was always far too busy to spend much time with Liza. Arthur Langley was a believer in the ''working vacation'' concept. ''You've got to come with us!'' Liza would implore, insisting that she'd go crazy alone, and eventually Tracy would relent.

It made sense, though, that Tracy, treasuring her privacy, would not reveal the true circumstances of these rather luxurious trips. Liza was reminded that no one in this entire town, except Tracy, was aware of her true identity. It was a delightful feeling, although at this particular moment it would have been far more comfortable to have this intimidating man look at her with some degree of respect. Instead he was ranting about the dangers awaiting reckless young females who wandered unescorted through the highways of Italy and France. "Look," she interjected hastily, "the last thing I want or need is a lecture from you, Mr.—"

"Van Cleef. Jacob Van Cleef." The voice was cool.

*I should have expected this,* Liza told herself now. *I should have guessed.*

"Aren't you going to ask me in?"

"Why?" Who did he think he was, anyway? This was the man who was trying to take the twins away from Tracy. This was the person who was hurting her dearest friend.

"Because I have certain matters to discuss with Tracy." He remained unperturbed.

Liza began to close the inside door. "Well, she isn't in right now."

A hand shot out and blocked the motion. "I'll wait then."

Was he just going to barge in like this? "Just a minute, Mr. Van Cleef!" She stood firmly in his way. "Tracy won't be back for several more hours."

He was uncomfortably close as the screen door slammed behind him. "I said, I'll wait."

Liza could scarcely believe his heavy-handed manner. "Who do you think you are, barging in here like you own the place?"

Jacob Van Cleef loomed incredibly tall over her as they stared at each other in the kitchen. "As it happens, I *do* own the place."

Liza was nonplussed. "You what?"

He seemed to enjoy her stunned reaction. "I own this house. I own the land around it." There was a significant pause. "I own many things."

"Including people?"

"Occasionally." The reply was delivered without a trace of humor. He stood even closer now, and for the first time it dawned on Liza that there were gold flecks in the brown eyes. She'd never met a man with gold flecks in his eyes—at least not that she'd bothered to notice. Involuntarily, she swallowed. The house suddenly seemed very warm.

"Do I make you nervous?" came the smooth inquiry.

"Certainly not," she retorted without much conviction.

Jacob Van Cleef gave an arrogant shrug and sauntered past her toward the worn sofa in the living room. He eased down on it, stretching out his long, lean legs. Liza simply gaped at him in mute outrage as he reached in his jacket pocket for a pack of cigarettes.

"Would you care for one?" he asked with irritating politeness.

"No." Her voice was an icicle. What was this man doing? Did he intend to sit here and make himself at home for the rest of the afternoon? And did he actually expect her to stand here and make small talk with him?

He drew out a plastic lighter and casually lit a cigarette, taking a long, deliberate drag. "So, Liza," he inquired with annoying familiarity, "how long do you plan to be visiting here amongst us rubes and hayseeds?" There was a biting edge to his sarcasm.

"My plans are my own affair," Liza responded tightly.

He inclined his head, undisturbed by her short tone. "Just trying to make polite conversation." He paused, then added, "something that is obviously beyond you, city girl."

Here Jacob Van Cleef managed to strike a vulnerable chord. Liza had always prided herself on her impeccable manners. At least, until today she had. It irked her to be subtly remonstrated by this . . . this person! "Won't you please excuse me, Mr. Van Cleef," she said with painstaking courtesy. "I must go upstairs and change into more appropriate attire."

Once more those enigmatic dark eyes raked her scantily clad body. "Not on my account," he murmured with a half smile. "And the name is Jacob."

"Yes, well," she stammered awkwardly, "please excuse me." Quickly, Liza left the room and retreated to the attic. What on earth had just happened down there? What demon had possessed her? No man had ever reduced her to an insecure, nervous mass of jelly before. When that overzealous newspaper reporter had confronted her with photographic evidence of Mark's "extracurricular" activities she had been stunned and hurt. Later on she'd been angry and embarrassed. But those feelings were nothing compared to her visceral reaction to Jacob Van Cleef.

Did the man have to be so incredibly attractive? No, wait. He wasn't attractive. Not really. Her mind was simply playing tricks on her, that was all. Sure, Liza assured herself as she slipped into her faded jeans and a pink T-shirt. It had something to do with being on the rebound from Mark. She recalled a well-known television psychologist once explaining how shattered love affairs left a person unusually vulnerable.

Liza examined her flushed face in the oval mirror. That had to be the explanation. She was simply vulnerable since her broken engagement. After all, it had been scarcely a week since she'd returned the exquisite sapphire ring that had been in the Sheridan family since the revolutionary war. Yes, she was vulnerable all right, but Elizabeth Langley had held her own against far more fearsome types than Mr.

Van Cleef. There wasn't a man alive who was capable of reducing *her* to a stutter.

But somehow Liza couldn't help but hope that when she finally returned downstairs, Jacob Van Cleef would be long gone.

# Chapter Three

Liza considered the next half hour one of the most awkward intervals she'd ever experienced. While she stared at the same page of magazine advertisement in a vain attempt to appear occupied, Jacob Van Cleef sat silently across the room, blowing smoke rings. As Liza reread the blurb about cold water laundry detergent for the nineteenth time, she could feel those dark eyes drilling into her.

Suddenly the man in the faded armchair cleared his throat. "I guess we aren't much on small talk, are we?" He crushed another cigarette in the ashtray.

"I guess not," came Liza's low reply. What on earth was the matter with her, anyway? Small talk had always been her forte. Liza Langley, the perfect young hostess who could talk to an endless succession of strangers about anything. Here she was with just another stranger, but in this particular situation she didn't *want* to talk. And it was obvious he was beginning to feel a bit uncomfortable as well. Where the heck was Tracy? If she didn't come walking through that door pretty soon, Liza was going to have to start talking about the weather. Wonderful!

"So what do you do in Washington?" the unwelcome visitor's deep voice punctuated the stillness once again.

"What do you mean?" Liza's tone was a trifle defensive.

He raised an eyebrow. "Just what I said—what do you do? Are you still in school?"

"No."

"Then I assume you must work." He paused. "What kind of work do you do?"

*None of your business,* she wanted to shout. In truth, though, Liza realized the question was no less intrusive now than the hundreds of times it had been asked by other acquaintances. It was just that everything that came out of the man's mouth seemed to annoy her. Maybe it had nothing to do with who he was. Perhaps any man would irritate her the same way right now because of her bitterness and anger at Mark Sheridan. And what difference did it make? It was obvious that Jacob Van Cleef was determined to have a conversation with her, no matter how one-sided. What would it cost her to go along with his superficial chatter?

"Are you a secretary?" Jacob Van Cleef continued his casual inquiry.

"No." For a moment, Liza was unsure what her answer should be. In truth, she didn't really know what kind of job she had. It had been difficult work, always being there for her father and, later on, for Mark. Organizing, arranging, making sure that the endless parade of social engagements went smoothly. Liza never thought of it as a job, it was merely what she *did*. The perfect hostess—she had never been anything else. That's what she was.

"A hostess." It took a few seconds for Liza to realize she had spoken the words aloud.

"What kind of restaurant?"

Liza put down the magazine. "Excuse me?"

He shrugged. "The place where you're a hostess. What kind of restaurant is it?"

"I don't work in a res—" Liza began indignantly, then stopped. Why should she correct the man's erroneous impression? What did it matter where Jacob Van Cleef thought she worked? Anyway, how could Liza even begin to explain her position as one of Washington's most prominent diplomatic hostesses without revealing her true identity? If during all these years Tracy hadn't seen fit to shed any light on her experiences with the Langleys with the people of Half Moon Falls, well then Liza wasn't going to, either.

Besides, Liza didn't exactly feel like discussing her private affairs with anyone in this hick town. The purpose of this little vacation was to get away from everything—the stress and the scrutiny. Good. Let Mr. Van Cleef think she was a waitress in a cocktail bar, for all she cared. As long as she could spend the next few weeks being anybody *except* Liza Langley of the Washington, Palm Beach and Park Avenue Langleys, it didn't matter what Jacob Van Cleef believed. In fact, Liza couldn't have asked for a more satisfactory turn of events.

"What kind of a restaurant is it?" the man prodded for a third time, the most subtle hint of suspicion in his voice. "Is there some reason you're reluctant to mention it by name?"

Liza could barely suppress a smile of amusement. What did this inquisitor suspect she was hiding? Did he have the kind of lurid imagination that allowed him to believe she might be ashamed or embarrassed about her place of employment? A number of images immediately came to mind—certain District of Columbia establishments of a somewhat dubious reputation. Liza was momentarily indignant. Is *that* what Jacob Van Cleef might be implying? That she worked in some kind of sleazy nightclub or, perhaps, even in a topless bar? "Not at all." Liza managed a cool retort, hastily mentioning the name of an extremely staid if not mediocre steak house on K Street. After all, if a person was going to lie about something, she should at least try to stick to the truth with as many details as possible.

"So how long are you going to be with us in Half Moon Falls?" her companion asked, repeating his earlier question.

Liza shrugged. "A few weeks—a month, perhaps. I'm not really sure."

Van Cleef stared at her thoughtfully. "Is that so?"

She quirked her eyebrow. "Do I have your permission?"

He gave a low laugh. "You have my permission." There was a pause. "What happened? Did you quit your job?"

Liza began to tap her foot impatiently. "Why would you think I've quit my job?"

Jacob Van Cleef uncrossed his lanky legs and looked directly at her. "Because it strikes me as rather unusual for the management to let an employee take an indefinite vacation. Unless—" his eyes were frankly curious "—that employee has absolutely no intention of returning."

Without a doubt this man had to be the nosiest human being she'd ever encountered, Liza fumed inwardly. Could any conversation be more exasperating than this one? But for Tracy's sake she wasn't going to lose her temper. Instead she gave a thin smile. "Actually, Mr. Van Cleef, the restaurant is currently undergoing extensive renovation. Like everyone else on the staff, I've been temporarily laid off. And like everyone else on the staff, I'll be returning to work once those renovations are complete. Does this sufficiently answer your question?"

A flash of humor flickered across his gaunt features. "Yes, it answers my question. But I thought you'd agreed to call me Jacob."

Liza studied those features for a long, unexpected moment. He was actually quite good-looking, she thought. Not all-American-boy handsome the way Mark was, but something indefinable. She didn't realize she had been staring until the tall visitor said softly, "Do you see something you like?"

"What?" Liza was momentarily flustered.

"I only ask because until this precise instant, I thought everything about me irritated you, Liza."

She tried to conceal her utter amazement. Had Jacob Van Cleef actually been so perceptive? Was he some kind of psychic or mind reader? Liza felt almost—what was the word?—*invaded*. For heaven's sake, what was keeping Tracy? She cleared her throat. "I beg your pardon, Mr. Van Cleef?"

"Jacob." It wasn't an order, it was a request.

"Fine—" she gave a shrug "—Jacob." At the moment Liza would have agreed to call him Humpty Dumpty if he would just stop looking at her with those incredibly penetrating eyes.

"Do I still irritate you?" he probed gently.

"Yes."

"What do you suggest I do about that?" He took several steps toward her in the small living room, and it made him seem to tower above her.

"Don't take it personally," Liza remarked blithely. "I'm sure you irritate everybody."

He twisted his lips. "You don't have a very high opinion of me, Liza."

"Do you really care what I think, Mr.—Jacob?"

"Yes, I do." There was no cynicism in his tone now. He actually seemed sincere.

Liza threw up her hands. "But you don't even know me!"

"Don't I?" For a moment there was silence, which was just as suddenly shattered by the slamming of a car door. The sound of childish laughter poured into the room as Tommy and Gary MacBride bounded wildly up the porch steps, threw open the screen door and careened into a rather hideous old lamp perched on one of the end tables. The fringed lamp shade shook violently, then the entire fixture toppled to the floor with a loud crash before anyone had a chance to react.

"Oh, *great,* you guys!" Tracy cried, entering the house right on the boys' heels and staring at the shattered remnants of the lamp strewn around her.

Tommy seemed contrite, but Gary shrugged at his older sister. "Oh, c'mon, Trace, it was ugly anyway!"

Tracy crossed her arms. "It was ugly, but it was the only lamp in this part of the room." She paused. "I hope you'll like sitting in the dark, both of you!"

"But Trace, it was just an ugly—" Tommy cast a supportive glance at his twin.

"I don't care—" Tracy began and stopped. For the first time since entering the house she seemed to notice Liza and the tall visitor.

Jacob gave a disparaging glance at the broken lamp, and his jaw tightened. "This is exactly what I mean," he said to Tracy. "This is precisely what I have been talking to you about for the past four months."

Never had Liza seen such a reaction on Tracy's face. Not in the entire five years of their friendship had Tracy's placid features hardened into such coldness. "I don't care to discuss this right now, Jake," Tracy said with obvious, barely suppressed, anger.

The chill in her voice didn't even appear to register on Jacob Van Cleef. He shook his head at the two boys. "Inside a home is not the place for rough-housing, and both of you know that."

His stern tone had a chastening effect on Tommy and Gary, who both hung their heads dejectedly. "We're sorry, Uncle Jake," they murmured in unison.

"Don't apologize to me," the man retorted. "Apologize to your sister."

"We're sorry, Trace—" the twins began and were quickly cut off.

"Jake—" Tracy's tone was icy "—I can discipline my own brothers."

"Is that so?" He drew another cigarette from his pocket. "From where I stand, you don't seem to be doing a very good job."

"I don't recall asking you," came the cold reply.

Liza didn't know whether to leave the room or remain where she was. All she knew was that this verbal exchange between her friend and Jacob Van Cleef was making her distinctly uncomfortable. Uncomfortable in a completely different way than when she'd been alone with the man. That sensation had been awkward but not altogether unpleasant. Now, however, something disagreeable and worrisome hovered in the air. Liza didn't like it. Not one bit.

Jacob sighed. "When are you going to behave sensibly about this, Tracy?"

"I already said, I don't care to discuss it now." The younger woman's retort was brittle. This was another side to Tracy, a side Liza had never known existed.

"You never want to discuss it; that's exactly the problem."

"This is none of your business, Jake," Tracy shot back angrily.

There was a strange silence. "Shall we discuss *that*, too?" the man asked. And in five quiet words the expression on Tracy's face had transformed. The harsh glitter in her eyes grew dull and lifeless.

"Gary," she uttered softly, "get the broom. Tommy, you get the dustpan."

"But we don't wanna have to—" they began to protest.

*"Now!"* There was more firmness and authority in the word than Liza had heard Tracy use with her

brothers. Sensitive to atmosphere and the note of command in their sister's voice, the twins scurried off in the direction of the kitchen.

Jacob waited till they had disappeared from the living room. He took a slow, deliberate drag on his cigarette. "This can't go on, Tracy. Sooner or later something is going to have to be done."

"I'll manage just fine, thank you." But her voice was oddly strained.

Jacob ignored her. "Let's leave out, for the moment, any financial considerations, shall we? Tommy and Gary, merely from a behavioral standpoint, would be a handful in a normal, two-parent family. Even your aunt and uncle had their work cut out for them. The sad fact is, they let the boys run wild." He caught the stricken expression on Tracy's face and added more gently, "I don't mean to speak ill of the dead, Tracy, but you know that's the truth. Lorna and Ray never spanked the twins once in their entire lives, and I can think of at least seven hundred times when either or both of them deserved a spanking."

"I can manage them just fine," Tracy repeated firmly.

"That's what you say now, Tracy," Jacob observed, extinguishing his cigarette. "But what happens a year or so from now when you've lost all your vitality? What happens when you start to resent them just a little?"

"I could never resent them. They're my brothers. I love them more than anything in the world."

Liza sensed something pained in Jacob's normally granite expression, and it surprised her. There were strange crosscurrents in the room. In some odd way she knew there were two levels to this conversation. Something unspoken lay just beneath the surface.

"I know you love them. I'm not saying you don't." He seemed to be choosing his words carefully. "They're good boys, Tracy, but they need a tight rein. How can you manage all that and still have a life of your own?"

"You're not taking Tommy and Gary away from me," Tracy said, sharply shaking her head.

"Nobody's trying to take the twins away from you." Jacob gave a weary sigh. "We just want to help you, Tracy."

"I don't want anybody's help."

"Fine!" the man threw his hands up in resignation. "Be proud and be stubborn. You aren't doing yourself or the twins a favor, believe me."

"This conversation is over," Tracy responded, her voice barely audible. She turned to Liza with a forced smile and handed her the keys to the Mustang. "Thanks for letting me use the car, Liz. It still runs like a charm."

"Sure." Liza couldn't think of anything else to say. And Jacob Van Cleef just stood there, as tall and towering as ever, staring back and forth between the women.

"Liza," he said finally, "talk to her. Maybe *you* can make your friend see common sense. Somebody has to." Without another word he turned and walked out of the house. Moments later they could hear the sound of his pickup truck pulling out of the gravel driveway.

"Damn," Tracy muttered, and plopped down on the couch.

Liza placed her hands on her hips and stared down at her best friend. "Okay, so *now* are you going to tell me what this is all about?"

"I can't."

Liza gave a low whistle. "Oh, c'mon, Trace. I think we're beyond all that by now."

"I suppose you're right," Tracy conceded reluctantly.

"Of course I'm right. I'm always right." Liza sat down on the other end of the lumpy, worn sofa and put her feet up on the battered coffee table. "Shoot."

"I'm not sure where to begin, Liz."

"How about at the beginning?"

Tracy ran a nervous hand through her unruly red hair. "Okay. When I was twelve, I moved here from the city with my mom and dad."

Liza looked at her in surprise. "But I thought—"

"That I was born in Half Moon Falls?" Her friend shook her head. "I guess you assumed that because I never talked much about my childhood. Actually I hated living in the city even more than this place, but that's another story. Anyway, my mom wanted to move here because she had relatives here, and my dad could never keep a job." Tracy stared blankly into the fireplace. "We lived in this ramshackle old house on the other side of town. I remember my folks started fighting a lot. Sometimes my dad would take off and not come back for weeks at a time. By the time Mom had the twins, Dad had taken off for good."

"I'm sorry, Trace," Liza murmured softly.

"Forget it. The point is, my mom didn't seem all that upset. Eventually she'd leave me alone with the babies at night and disappear somewhere. Later on, I found out—" Tracy stopped suddenly. "I really hate talking about this, Liz, so I'm going to make it pretty brief. My mom was having an affair with the richest, meanest man in town: Jacob Van Cleef, *Senior*."

Liza raised an eyebrow. "Jake's father?"

"Right." Tracy continued to gaze into the fireplace. "But it wasn't until long after my mom died, and later on, when Van Cleef, Senior died, too, that I found out from my Aunt Lorna that—" She stopped.

"Finish it, Trace," Liza prompted gently. She had already guessed the end of the story. It should have been obvious long ago.

"There's a strong probability that Van Cleef was the father of Tommy and Gary," Tracy blurted out.

"And that would mean Jake is—"

"The twins' half brother." There was bitter pain in Tracy's words. "Don't you see why I'm so worried? As a close relative, Jake can sue me for custody!"

Liza touched her friend's hand in a comforting gesture. "Believe me, Trace, it's not that easy. He'd have to prove you an unfit guardian."

"No, he wouldn't," Tracy disagreed. "All Jake has to prove is that he'd be a *better* guardian. Let's get a dose of reality, here. If he can establish his blood ties to Tommy and Gary, Jake probably has the same legal rights to them as *I* do."

"You don't know that for sure. I'll bet you haven't even seen a lawyer about this."

"That's not the point. If this goes to court, I'll lose the boys for sure. No judge around here is going to turn down a Van Cleef." There was an uncomfortable pause. "And why should he? I know Jake can give the twins everything they need, things I can't afford to give them."

"Money isn't everything," Liza interjected. *And I ought to know,* she thought caustically.

"Oh, that's not all," her friend reasoned. "The judge will probably believe that boys need a father figure for a positive male role model. And maybe he'd be right. Oh, damn! Maybe I *don't* know what's best for the kids, Liz. Maybe I'm being selfish about wanting to keep them."

"You're not selfish," Liza countered. "You love your brothers. All you're trying to do is keep your family together. Is that so bad?"

"I'm beginning to wonder." Tracy glanced purposefully at her wristwatch. "Well, I guess I'd better take a shower and get ready."

"Oh, do you have a date?" Liza was apologetic. "I hope I'm not in the way."

"What on earth are you talking about?" Tracy waved her hand. "I've got to get ready for work."

Liza was surprised. "Work? But I thought the school year was over."

"It is over. I'm talking about my other job, my evening job, over at the Fralinglitch Inn. Saturday is always our busiest night."

"Oh." Liza paused. "Listen, if it's just a matter of money—"

"Forget it. I know what you're going to say and just forget it."

"How do you know what I'm going to say?" she protested.

"C'mon, Liz. We know each other too well." Tracy rose from the sofa. "You've been trying to get me to take money for years. Understand me. You're my best friend, but I'll never take a cent from you."

"Why? I don't see the point."

"I don't want to argue about this. It's the way I feel, the way I've always felt about it."

Liza was tempted to throw a pillow at her. "Agh, sometimes you're so stubborn!"

Tracy sighed. "Now you sound just like Jake."

"Oh, *please!*"

"Look, Liz. The truth is, you came here to get away from things for a while. I might not be all that keyed up about *living* here, but Half Moon Falls can be a pretty nice place to visit. There isn't a nightlife to speak of, but you might find the days serene. I'll bet you haven't even seen the falls yet."

"No, I haven't."

"The point is, I feel kind of crummy about being busy while you're here. I'm not much of a hostess—"

"Please, that *word!*" Liza groaned.

# Chapter Four

Before Liza went to bed that night she decided to call her father. After she and the twins had dinner, a casserole that had been efficiently prepared in advance by Tracy, Liza had spent the next three hours playing with the boys. She wondered where two creatures could come up with such an endless supply of energy. She also began to wonder if Jacob Van Cleef had spoken the truth when he expressed his concern to Tracy. In just one short evening, Tommy and Gary's childish exuberance had left her exhausted. What must it be like for Tracy, regardless of all her good intentions?

"Jake is taking us fishing tomorrow," Tommy reminded his brother for the sixteenth time.

"Do you want to see the fishing rods he bought us for Christmas?" Gary asked ingenuously.

"That would be nice." Liza gave him a groggy smile.

"He didn't give us them for Christmas. It was our birthday," Tommy remarked with youthful superiority.

"Uh-uh," Gary retorted. "Uncle Jake gave us the bikes on our birthday."

"That was Christmas."

"Was not."

"Was too."

"Wanna bet?"

"Yeah!" Tommy gave a smirk. "Sometimes you're so stupid!"

"Well, you're stupider!" His twin gave him a playful punch, and moments later the two boys were tussling on the living-room floor.

"Cut it out, you two," Liza said, finally managing to pull the youngsters apart—a difficult task because they clung to each other like leeches.

"Aw, we're just playin', Liz!" Gary protested.

"Nevertheless, you might have hurt each other."

"What's *nevertheless*?" Tommy inquired.

"Forget it." Liza rolled her eyes. "Don't you guys ever get tired?" Gracious, poor Tracy. How on earth *did* she manage to keep her sanity?

Finally the youngsters went upstairs to bed, and Liza called her father collect in Washington.

"I've been worried sick about you, Liza," the gravelly voice that had intimidated many a foreign diplomat crackled over the wire. "How could you just leave like that without a word?"

"I had to get away, Dad. You know that."

"I'll say this again, my dear. Mark Sheridan can kiss his political future farewell," her father asserted harshly.

"Do we have to talk about that?" Liza protested. "I'm tired of hearing it already."

"His career is over, sweetheart. I'll never forgive him for making a fool out of you!"

"Please, Dad!" She rolled her eyes. "I didn't call to listen to this. I just want you to know that I'm staying with Tracy for a while, and everything is fine."

"Are you sure?" Arthur Langley's tone grew less pompous and more subdued. "If I didn't have this summit conference coming up in Vienna, I'd take you on a trip, just you and me."

Liza recognized the tinge of regret in his words, but the sad truth was her father would never have the time for just the two of them. She had never resented this state of affairs, simply accepting it as the price of being the daughter of a great man. There would always be something more important to demand Arthur Langley's attention: a revolution in Africa, a crisis in the Persian Gulf.... "It's okay," she said honestly. After all, how could a broken romance compete with a world disarmament conference? "As I told you, with a little time and distance I'll be just fine."

"Good." Ambassador Langley seemed relieved. "I never really doubted that. You're a sensible girl, and these things will pass, believe me." He cleared his throat. "Well, my dear, take care of yourself." Deep emotion always made her father distinctly uncomfortable, and Liza knew it was time to draw the phone call to a close. "If you need anything, anything at all—"

She sighed knowingly. "I'll get in touch with you or someone at the house." For some unexplained reason, tears started to mist in her eyes. Here she stood in Tracy's tiny kitchen, feeling dreadfully alone. Isolated. Apart from everything and everybody. "Well, good luck at the conference."

"We'll need it, sweetheart." Arthur Langley paused. "Good night, Liza."

"Good night, Dad." Slowly, with the slightest touch of disappointment, she replaced the receiver on the wall. Heading toward the stairs, Liza paused in the living room to pick up a paperback book from the hundreds piled on the corner shelves. She didn't even look at the title. It didn't seem to matter. Then she trudged wearily upstairs to bed.

The strain of all the hard work and long hours must have gotten to Tracy, or perhaps she'd simply decided to sleep late. In any event, Tommy and Gary were a great example of a human alarm clock, Liza thought as she sat at the kitchen table with the youngsters, all three of them eating bowls of cold cereal and discussing fish.

"Last time I caught a trout," remarked Tommy.

"I caught three," topped his sibling.

"Just lucky." Tommy shrugged and turned his attention to the door. "That's Uncle Jake's truck!"

Self-consciously Liza put her hand to her disheveled hair. She wasn't wearing a trace of makeup and her feet were bare. She quickly reassured herself that it didn't matter if Jacob Van Cleef saw her this way; it was simply a matter of pride. Liza always liked to look her best. The front door slammed. Gracious, didn't the man believe in knocking?

Moments later he hovered over her in the tiny kitchen. "Good morning, Liza." There was a pause as Jacob took in her appearance. "Did you sleep well?"

"Very." Liza swallowed a mouthful of cold cereal with as much aplomb as she could muster. She had to admit the man was devastatingly attractive this morning. There was nothing deliberate or contrived about the way he dressed. Just as yesterday, Jacob's clothes were relaxed and casual, a natural extension of himself, from the faded plaid shirt and khaki fishing vest to the worn denims hugging his lanky frame. She couldn't help but remember the calculated way Mark fussed with his clothes, his tie always perfectly tied, and never a hair out of place. What a contrast, Liza thought bitterly.

"You're staring again," Jacob said quietly. "I can't imagine what you find so fascinating."

"I wasn't staring."

"Fine. Whatever you say." There was an awkward silence. "Tell me, Liza. Do you always look this good in the morning?"

"You've got to be kidding!"

The man was genuinely puzzled. "Why would I be kidding?" He settled into the chair next to her. "So are you coming with us?"

She stared at him. "I beg your pardon?"

"Have you ever been fishing?"

"No."

He grinned unexpectedly, and the change in his usually harsh features made him seem years younger. "You'd enjoy it. I wish you'd come along."

Liza shook her head. "No, thank you."

"Why not?"

"Let's just say that I don't think it would be such a good idea."

"I think it's a terrific idea." Jacob rocked back on the chrome and vinyl kitchen chair. Like everything else in the room, the bright aqua furniture was right out of the 1950s. "It'll be fun. I'll teach you how to fish."

"Really," she insisted uncomfortably, "I'd rather not."

"Wait a second—" he continued to rock back on the rear legs of the chair, ignoring the teetering motion "—did I tell you I brought sandwiches? And not only did I bring them but I made them myself. Do you like roast beef on those hard rolls with the little seeds on top, Liza?"

She looked at him in astonishment. Arrogant Jacob Van Cleef actually sounded like a little kid getting all excited about a picnic lunch! "It sounds very nice, but—"

"Oh, and there are chocolate brownies—"

Liza shook her head. "I appreciate your asking me along, but as I said, it wouldn't be a good idea."

"And you still haven't said why." The smile slowly left his face, which became a granite mask again. "Wait, let me guess. You probably figure it would be fraternizing with the enemy."

"I never said that."

"You didn't have to." The chair slammed down on all four legs. "But that's just what you were thinking, wasn't it?"

"Look," she pleaded, "I'd rather not get into an argument over this."

He shrugged. "Who's arguing? I'm just stating a fact." Jacob's gaze was frank. "It's true, isn't it?"

"Well," Liza conceded, "let's just say it places me in a somewhat awkward position." Tracy *was* her best friend, after all. Going out on a fishing expedition with a man who was supposedly her arch enemy did strike Liza as disloyal.

He gave a resigned sigh. "You know, Liza, there are two sides to every story."

She shook her head again. "That may well be, but one of those sides belongs to my dearest friend."

"Your friend is one of the proudest, most obstinate, pigheaded young women I have ever known in my entire life!"

"That may be true, but she is still my dearest friend."

"Well," Jacob countered, "then maybe you can get her to listen to you."

"She's never listened to me before," Liza tossed back bluntly. "I doubt she'd start listening now."

Her companion leaned over the table, his hard, tanned face close to hers. "And what do *you* think, Liza? Do you think I'm some kind of ogre?"

"I don't know you well enough to formulate an opinion."

"Spoken like a true politician."

"Oh, that word!" Liz rolled her eyes.

"What's wrong with it?" He glanced at her vaguely.

"Never mind, it's all rather involved," she said hastily.

"In any event, allow me to disagree with your previous statement. I happen to believe you know me much better than you might care to admit."

"What an odd thing to say." Liza stared at him questioningly. "I only met you yesterday."

"Then why do I feel as if I've known you for a very long time?" There was a strange note to his voice. "And why do I get the distinct impression that even though you'd prefer to dislike me, you really don't dislike me at all, Liza?''

There he went again—reading her mind! This was getting to be absurd. Weren't a person's thoughts supposed to be her own? How could this near-stranger always know what she was thinking? Mark Sheridan had known her far longer, yet he'd never been able to guess what was on Liza's mind. In retrospect, there was something so comfortingly safe and secure in keeping one's thoughts private. Mark had never invaded that space. And even if he'd possessed the ability to do so, Liza doubted her ex-fiancé would have wished to. He was too wrapped up in his own concerns to care or wonder what was on her mind. Like most people, Mark was far more at ease on a more superficial level. Her attention was drawn back to Jacob. He seemed to be waiting for her to say something.

"I don't dislike you."

"Well," he reasoned, "that's a start, anyway. With enough time and patience, I might even get you to *like* me." It was difficult to tell if the man was joking or not. The two of them seemed to be walking a fine line between levity and substance.

"We put all our stuff in the back of the truck, Uncle Jake!" Gary and Tommy bounded into the room again, a dual whirlwind of incredible energy. "What kind of sandwiches did you bring this time?"

"Roast beef." He regarded them good-naturedly. "Where are your jackets?"

"Do we have to have 'em?"

Jacob gave a firm nod. "It might get chilly later on. Go upstairs and get them."

Without another word of protest the brothers obediently ran off on their errand. It was obvious that both Tommy and Gary regarded Jacob Van Cleef with a combination of awe and affection. And it was also apparent that his interest in the twins went beyond a mere sense of responsibility. Evidently he was quite fond of the boys, despite his tirade of the day before. If there ever was a man full of contradictions, here was the one, Liza mused.

"I accept defeat this time," Jacob murmured softly, "But one of these days, I *will* take you on a picnic."

"Perhaps," she responded evasively, unwillingly admitting to herself that the idea of going anywhere with Jacob Van Cleef was at once disturbing yet fascinating.

When Tracy finally woke, Liza discovered that Sunday was Tracy's one day of rest. She also discovered that Sunday, coincidentally, was the day that Jacob always took the twins somewhere.

"I suppose I should be grateful for him taking the boys off my hands on my day off, but I don't *feel* like being grateful," Tracy grumbled that afternoon during lunch.

"You know," Liza began tentatively, "I believe he truly cares for the twins."

There were lines under Tracy's eyes. "Do you think I don't know that, Liz?"

"Why do you hate him?"

"It shows, huh?" Tracy gave a bitter smile. "I didn't always hate the guy. In fact, I kind of looked up to him when I was a kid. He was one of the few people in this town who acted nice to me."

"What went wrong?"

Tracy's eyes clouded. "I know you've seen the pictures on my old dresser. Peter Van Cleef was a senior in high school when I was a junior." Her voice trembled. "I've never met anybody else like him, Liz. He was so sweet and gentle. From the time I moved to Half Moon Falls, we were best friends. I was such a tomboy back then, it was hard for some people to remember I was actually a girl. Anyway, when I turned sixteen I suddenly stopped wanting to be a tomboy. All at once I was doing weird stuff, like curling my hair and becoming a cheerleader." Her voice drifted off.

"What happened, Trace?" Liza prodded her gently.

"Very simple. One day Peter looked at me and was glad I'd stopped being a tomboy. He took me to the Senior Dance, and everything changed overnight. Needless to say, his family was not amused. After all," she murmured caustically, "while I was just one of the boys, I wasn't a threat to the exalted Van Cleefs, but as a girlfriend for Peter I wasn't good enough. It was an embarrassment to them, you can well imagine, Liza. The daughter of the old man's one-time mistress thinking she could aspire to the son of the manor. I didn't expect them to welcome me with open arms. The only other person I thought would be in my corner was Jake. He'd never seemed snobby like the rest of his family.'' She shook her head in disbelief.

"But all of a sudden, there he was, determined to break us up. I remember it so well, Liz. The look on his face was so *cold*. Anyway, Peter idolized his big brother. I guess he probably figured if Jake didn't think I was good enough, then perhaps I wasn't. We stopped going out after that.'' Her voice quivered again. ''That summer his family packed him off to Europe. By the time fall came around he was already enrolled in a university in California.''

''Where is he now, Trace?'' Liza wanted to know.

''Still out on the West Coast,'' her friend replied tonelessly. ''I understand he got married last year.''

It was difficult for Liza to believe that anyone could have been so cruel to Tracy. It was equally baffling that such a person could be Jacob Van Cleef. He might be dictatorial and arrogant—that much was true—but he didn't seem like a heartless human being. Then Liza was forced to remind herself that if the past two weeks had taught her anything, it was that she had been wrong about men before. It certainly wasn't farfetched to think she could make such a critical error again.

## Chapter Five

Jacob didn't get out of his truck when he dropped the boys off at home later that afternoon. It was almost as if he knew his presence wouldn't be welcome. Liza felt a mixture of disappointment and relief. There was little doubt that she was strangely drawn to Jacob Van Cleef. And in some ways it was a welcome feeling after the jarring numbness of the past few weeks. For once someone other than Mark Sheridan was occupying her thoughts. So what if this man made her feel uncomfortable? She had to admit that discomfort was preferable to pain any day of the week.

She looked forward to the chance for another conversation with Jacob. It was difficult to keep reminding herself that he was also cast in the role of

Tracy's nemesis. Something was going to have to be done about that, Liza decided. Sooner or later, Jake and Tracy would have to reach some kind of armistice, if only for the sake of Tommy and Gary. Tracy would have to put her bitterness behind her and attempt to forgive and forget. And Jacob Van Cleef would have to face the fact that he couldn't run roughshod over everyone else's lives. The idea of getting two such incredibly stubborn people to reach some sort of compromise reminded Liza of one of the awesome diplomatic negotiations her father was often called on to perform.

"Uncle Jake says if it's okay with you, he wants to send us to camp this summer!" Gary bubbled excitedly to his big sister.

"Oh, *does* he?" Tracy's eyes narrowed.

"Say we can go, Trace," Tommy implored. "They've got canoe races and everything!"

"How wonderful."

The boys exchanged disappointed glances. "Told you she'd say no," Tommy informed his brother. "'Cause she's still mad at Uncle Jake."

"She didn't say no," Gary considered. "Did you, Trace?"

"I haven't said anything," his sister informed him coolly. "Now go upstairs and wash up. It's dinnertime."

Dejectedly the boys trudged toward the hallway. "Look at this—" Tracy pointed to a Styrofoam cooler by the door "—they were so thrilled about the prospect of summer camp, they didn't even brag about the fish they caught." She ran tense fingers through her curly hair. "Damn, Liz! How can I compete with summer camp and bicycles?"

Liza hesitated. "Who says you have to?"

"What do you mean? Of course I have to."

"I don't understand, Trace. Why do you see this as some kind of competition?"

"Because it is!" her friend's voice rose in frustration.

"It doesn't have to be." Liza crossed her arms. "Do you think the boys are going to love you any less because you can't give them as many things as Jacob?"

There was an awkward pause. "He won't rest until he's taken them away from me."

"Is that your only reason, Trace?"

"What's that supposed to mean?"

"I think you're letting an old grudge get in the way of what's best for Tommy and Gary."

"A *grudge*! Is that what you'd call it?"

Liza stared her friend directly in the eye. "It doesn't matter what you call it. Call it anything you like—the end result remains the same. What Jacob did to you was cruel and inexcusable, but the past is the past. Life goes on. You're not a vulnerable teenager any longer." She spoke with the calm yet forceful tone she'd so often heard her father use. "No one is saying you should forget the past or even forgive what happened. But that was between Jacob and you. The boys have nothing to do with it. Don't put them in the middle, Trace. It isn't fair.''

Tracy gave a weary sigh. "You think I should let them go, don't you?''

"All kids love camp.''

"I'm not talking about camp, Liz. You think I should let them *go*.''

"I never said that.''

"You don't have to.'' She paced back and forth across the living room. "You think it hasn't crossed my mind what it would mean for those little guys? They really adore Jake, and he could give them everything kids need when they're growing up— things I never had. It's just that—'' Tracy stared down at the floor ''—I'm so afraid.''

"What are you afraid of, Trace?'' Liza prodded her friend gently.

"Of being left out.'' There was a pause. "No, that's not exactly the word. I'm scared of being *shut* out.''

"For some reason,'' Liza murmured, "I don't think Jake would ever do that.''

"I wish I could believe you, Liz. Somehow, I just can't.''

Liza wished that Jacob and her dearest friend could declare a truce. Something had to be done to put an end to this bitter feud. And that's when an idea occurred to her: maybe she could help. After all, Liza Langley was a diplomat's daughter. She'd certainly poured enough oil over troubled waters in the past. Why was this situation any more difficult to resolve than any Liza had found herself caught in the middle of before? Besides, she'd dealt with greater egos in Washington that were no less bruised. Sure, Liza thought confidently. One way or another, everything always boiled down to diplomacy. Yes, getting these two stubborn mules to declare a truce would be quite a challenge....

"What are you thinking, Liz?"

"Oh," Liza said, smiling vaguely at Tracy, "nothing much."

For the next several days Liza decided not to broach the subject at all. She spent the time helping Tracy look after the twins and familiarizing herself with her surroundings. When Tracy wanted to talk, Liza listened and tried not to offer any opinion. Washington, D.C., and her own troubles somehow began to seem remote and unreal. As far as she was concerned this little trip was certainly serving its original purpose.

Liza had plenty of time for introspection. Tracy left the house every day by three-thirty for her job at the Fralinglitch Inn and didn't return home until well after midnight. By then she was so exhausted that Liza wished for once Tracy would break down and accept the financial help she had offered, but she knew she'd have more success talking to a brick wall.

For the first time in her life Liza began to question her own values. There had never been a time she'd been forced to struggle for the things she needed. If she ever expressed a desire for a car or clothes, these things were readily provided to her without protest or argument. If Liza chose to work, it was because work was an outlet for her energies, not because it put groceries on the table. She wasn't ashamed of being rich; it was the unfairness of things that troubled her.

In the middle of the week, when the twins were spending the night with friends and Tracy had already left for work, Liza received a phone call from Jacob Van Cleef.

"About that picnic," he began conversationally.

"I'd forgotten all about it," she replied.

"Be that as it may, I'm calling in my rain check."

"I don't recall having given you one."

"Well, it just goes to show you, Liza. Memory is an elusive thing." He paused. "What time shall I pick you up?"

"Excuse me?"

"I can be over there in half an hour."

"Now just a minute." She was nonplussed. "You want to go on a picnic *tonight*?"

Jacob hesitated. "I realize it's short notice, but I just got back into town a few minutes ago."

The short notice didn't actually disturb her at all. In truth, Liza had always been an impromptu person. "It's just that I thought picnics were for the daytime."

"Are you afraid of the dark, Liza?" His voice was deep.

"Not at all. It's just that—"

"Are you afraid of me?" There was an awkward silence.

"Whatever gave you such a ridiculous idea?"

"Then why don't I come by in about thirty minutes? You know you're dying to find out just how good my roast beef sandwiches really are." There was something so guileless in his tone that there was really no way Liza could refuse him. Not that she intended to.

"All right."

"Good." Jacob seemed quite pleased with himself. "Wear something comfortable. There might be some spray from the falls."

"The falls?"

"Don't tell me you haven't been over to the falls yet?" There was surprise in his tone.

"I hadn't gotten around to it, actually."

"Well, it's about time you did."

Liza spent the next half hour getting ready for her date with Jacob. A date—was *that* what it was? Strange, she hadn't even put such a word to it until just this moment. It had been well over a year since she'd gone out with any man other than Mark. On the other hand, perhaps this wasn't a date in the conventional meaning of the word. Perhaps Jacob was hoping to win her over as Tracy's best friend in an effort to enlist her help. That notion made a great deal of sense. Well, whatever the reason, a picnic with Jacob Van Cleef was the perfect venue for Liza's subtle negotiations. Her plans to engineer a truce between two extremely strong-willed adults had to begin somewhere.

Liza dressed for the first round of her negotiations with great care. The only other times the man had seen her, she'd been either haggard from exhaustion or disheveled from sleep. Since driving from Washington Liza hadn't even opened her makeup case. Now she made sure she looked her best, with an application of mascara and subtle blusher. Her blond hair fell in freshly brushed waves over a red-and-white striped sweater with a gentle scoop neck. The only item of Liza's wardrobe that remained the same at all times was her one pair of faded blue jeans.

Exactly thirty minutes from the time of his phone call Jacob appeared at the door. He was dressed in his familiar black windbreaker and slacks. He stared down at Liza from the doorway, his dark eyes traveling over her body in frank approval. "You look lovely."

"Thank you." She tried to sound casual, but his intense gaze was disconcerting. "Tommy and Gary are at a sleep-over party tonight," she explained hastily.

Jake nodded. "I know, down at little Joey Berger's house."

"Is there anything going on in this town that you *don't* know about?" Liza shook her head in wonderment.

"I already told you. I know everything," came the matter-of-fact response.

Moments later they were in the roomy cab of Jacob's pickup, bounding over a series of dirt roads. The cab smelled of tobacco and fruit, an odd combination. Every time the truck went over a bump, Liza slid at least a foot one way and then the other across the wide leather bench seat.

"If you wore your seat belt you wouldn't go bouncing around like that," her driver said disapprovingly.

"I'd wear it if I could find it." She cast a critical eye along the seat.

Jacob uttered something beneath his breath and immediately pulled over to the side of the road. Without a word he leaned across the length of the cab. Fumbling just for a moment along the backrest, he pulled up the missing ends of the safety harness. Reaching swiftly over her shoulder, he tightened one end of the belt, then clipped it firmly shut across her lap. His hands hesitated for a mere instant against Liza's waist, and she gave an involuntary tremor. "Is it comfortable?" he inquired with forced casualness.

"Fine. Thank you." Liza was unable to look him directly in the eye. For goodness' sake, all the man had done was adjust a seat belt! Why was she feeling so oddly off balance?

Jacob drew back suddenly and put the vehicle into gear. Not another word was spoken between them until the truck pulled down an incline leading to the falls. Although it was early evening, the late spring sun had not yet set. In the distance Liza could hear the ripple of a running stream.

"There isn't a road going down the rest of the way," Jacob explained. "I hope you don't mind a little bit of a walk." He reached behind him for a woven straw hamper and a neatly folded plaid blanket.

The narrow, winding path was rocky and occasionally difficult to maneuver. Jacob led the way with incredible ease, considering his large frame and the fact that both arms were occupied.

"I wish you'd let me carry something," Liza remarked, feeling somewhat guilty that her hands were free of any burden.

"Forget it," he said with a shrug. "Now, watch out over here. It gets a bit slippery."

Despite nearly losing her footing half-a-dozen times, Liza made it down to the end of the path without incident.

"So what do you think of Half Moon Falls?" Jacob asked quietly.

"It's beautiful." Liza just stood there, staring at the unexpectedly exquisite scenery.

"You sound surprised." He set the basket and blanket down.

"I am surprised." It was an honest response. Liza had traveled her entire life. She had seen the awesome wonder of the Himalayas and the incomparable splendor of Kuaui. In fact, having been all over the world, she had seen everything from the commonplace to the exotic. But here was such a simple beauty that it was impossible to remain unmoved. Several streams converged at one point, then splintered off into a series of shimmering cascades against a small, rocky cliff. One of the waterfalls bubbled down into a pool, overhung by graceful old elm trees.

"When the moon rises and its reflection floats in that pond, you'll see why they call this place Half Moon Falls," Jacob said behind her.

It seemed fitting that the sleepy little village that had initially impressed Liza as one of those tiny enchanted towns that disappear overnight in a fairy tale, would have such a storybook setting as this. The clear water bounced over the rocks with an almost divine resonance. "I'm glad we came here," she murmured softly. "Thank you for bringing me, Jacob."

"My pleasure," came the deep reply. But there was a subtle note of astonishment in his voice, as if he hadn't expected such a reaction.

They spread the large, woolen blanket by the water's edge and began to pull the dinner out of the picnic basket. Besides the homemade roast beef sandwiches on huge, hard rolls, he'd packed potato salad, pickles and moist, dark chocolate brownies with icing. "You certainly put a charming little dinner together at the last minute," Liza smiled.

He grinned back. "I cannot tell a lie. The potato salad and brownies are store-bought." There was also a bottle of red wine, which Jacob uncorked and poured into plastic cups.

The next few hours were so tranquil, so serene, that it was difficult for Liza to remember that several short days ago she had been so miserable. And the man who initially had seemed so unpleasant proved a delightful, entertaining dinner companion. Not wanting to talk about herself, Liza skillfully steered the conversation back to Jacob every time it threatened to meander too close to her life and experiences in Washington, D.C. Instead she learned more about the man who sat sprawled out on the blanket next to her. After serving with the U.S. forces in Vietnam, Jacob had returned to assume an active role in running the family dairy business.

"I suppose that might strike you as being a trifle dull," he said as he refilled their wine cups.

"Actually I find it very interesting," Liza remarked. This third refill of wine was making her feel pleasantly relaxed and light-headed.

He eyed her intently. "That's surprising, when you consider that Washington is a much more interesting place than Half Moon Falls."

"That depends on your perspective."

"And what kind of perspective is that, Liza?"

This conversation was starting to stray too close to home, and her discomfort was obvious. "Oh," she said quickly, "I just mean that when you live in a place for as long as I've lived in Washington, it tends to lose most of its mystique."

"So all that talk about our nation's capital being the 'nerve center of the world' doesn't carry much weight with you?" He quirked a curious eyebrow.

"I agree that Washington *is* the nerve center of the globe. I just don't happen to be particularly interested in politics." What a bald-faced lie, she chastised herself. If Arthur Langley could hear his daughter, his jaw would drop to the ground! She found politics exceedingly interesting; it was *politicians* Liza could do without right now—one handsome Midwestern senator in particular.

"I used to take quite an interest in our political system when I was younger," Jacob remarked quietly. "I even pursued a graduate degree in it." He ignored Liza's look of surprise. "You see, I thought I could help change things back then." There was a touch of irony to his words. "What can I say? I was young and idealistic. It was before your time, Liza, but in the sixties and early seventies it seemed we all had dreams of changing the world...making it a better place."

"And now?"

Jacob sipped his wine. "Now I have a more realistic philosophy: brighten up the corner where you are."

"I can't say I disagree with that point of view." Liza finished her glass. "It's great if you live in a place like this, but Washington has a *lot* of dark corners." She had no idea how bitter the words sounded until Jacob glanced at her sharply.

"Who hurt you, Liza?"

She stared at him blankly, astonished at the intensity of his question. "I don't know what you're talking about. I was speaking about things in general."

"It sounded rather specific to me." Jacob's brown eyes had an alien glitter. "I'll ask again. Who hurt you?"

"Nobody!" she practically shouted.

"Oh, *that's* convincing. Why don't you yell a little louder, and I'll really believe you." Jacob twisted his mouth. "What kind of man was he?"

"What man?" she avoided the heat of his stare.

"You know very well who I'm talking about." He reached over and took the empty cup from her hand.

"I d-don't want to talk about it," Liza stammered. "In fact, I was thinking that this is an excellent opportunity to bring up the subject of Tracy—"

"I don't want to talk about Tracy at the moment."

"And the twins."

Jacob placed two steadying hands on her shoulders. "I don't want to talk about the twins, either," he uttered harshly. "I want to talk about *you*, Liza. Just you."

The warmth generated by his hard fingers radiated through Liza's thin sweater. "There really isn't much to talk about," she retorted with false brightness.

"On the contrary, I believe it's a subject we can discuss at great length." He drew closer. "I know you're running away from something, Liza. I also know it can only be a man. You've had that wounded look ever since we met."

"Oh, thanks a lot!" She tried to sound indignant, but it was difficult when he was so close, touching her this way.

"If you don't want to talk about the man who hurt you enough to make you run away, fine. I won't press you right now. But I'll tell you this—" he lowered his gaunt face to hers "—I intend to make you forget him, Liza." Those hard hands traveled upward to clasp her flushed cheeks with incredible gentleness. Slowly he brought his lips down onto hers in a brief but electric contact. It was a kiss that made no demands, yet it was starkly evident that Jacob Van Cleef was staking his claim.

Liza pulled away quickly. "I didn't come here for this!"

"I'm not sure whether or not I believe you, honey."

"Whether or not you believe me doesn't really matter," she retorted hotly. "And don't call me *honey* again, Mr. Jacob Van Cleef!"

His eyes actually twinkled. "I suppose this is a good time for dessert. Would you care for a brownie?"

"No, I would *not* care for a brownie!"

"They're quite good, although not as good as the ones I bake. I'll bet you didn't know I'm an excellent brownie chef, Liza."

"Don't change the subject."

His eyes narrowed. "I thought you *wanted* me to change the subject. Isn't that what this is all about?"

"And don't you start *that* again!"

"Start what?"

"Pretending you can read my mind."

"Can't I?" All traces of levity had left his face. Jacob drew close again and grasped a strand of Liza's golden hair. "A beautiful setting for a beautiful girl. If you could read *my* mind, Liza, you would know that's what I'm thinking at this moment."

"I'd rather you didn't do this," she protested.

"Do what?" he murmured, running his fingers across the blond waves tumbling down her back.

"Don't play games with me, Jacob!"

"Who's playing games?" He continued the tantalizing caress. "Maybe those men you knew in Washington played games, but not me."

"Please stop." Liza wanted to pull away, but there was something hypnotic in the lazy motion of his fingers. It left her oddly disturbed and vulnerable. She didn't want to feel hypnotized by anybody.

"Do you know what else I'm thinking right now?" he continued, ignoring her protest. "I'm thinking that I ought to finish what I start. That was a sweet kiss, Liza, but it was over before it even began."

"Of all the conceited, arrogant—"

"Who's being conceited? I'm just stating a fact." He brought his hand from her hair to gently cup her chin and lowered his mouth to hers once again.

If it was another tender, undemanding kiss she had been expecting, Liza was completely taken off guard by this new assault on her senses. The pressure of his lips was intense and unrelenting, forcing a response. Liza's mouth parted in silent assent to his sensuous probing. His hot tongue urgently tasted the moist textures of her mouth. The sensation was drugging, intoxicating. She had been kissed many times before, but nothing compared to this—not Mark's expert and confident caresses, so physically intimate yet aloof at the same time. Jacob's kisses were different. Every point of contact was a shock…his hands on the small of her back, his chest pressed against hers, his lips that continued to savor the sweetness of her own. Each place their bodies touched seemed a link in a chain of fire.

Jacob gave a groan and pulled away to stare down at her flushed face. "You're driving me crazy, do you know that?"

"I don't know anything," she said unsteadily. "*You're* supposed to be the mind reader, remember?"

"Maybe I'm not such a terrific mind reader, after all." His brown eyes glimmered. "I never thought, even for a moment, that kissing you would be like this." He reached out and traced the outline of her lips with a proprietary finger. Then his finger began to travel down the line of her neck. The deliberate slowness of the gesture made Liza shiver involuntarily.

"What are you doing?" she whispered.

"Touching you, honey."

In the far recesses of Liza's brain little warning bells began to ring. She reached up and stilled his hand. "Stop." It was more a plea than a command.

"I can't help wanting to touch you," Jacob murmured insistently in her ear. "Why do you want me to stop?"

Liza shook her head mutely, overcome with a strange embarrassment. Kissing this man was quite unbelievably pleasurable, but now that she was free of his embrace, it was as if someone had poured the icy cold waters of reality over her. "I think we should be getting home."

"What's wrong?"

"Nothing's wrong." She cleared her throat. "It's just that it *is* getting late—"

"It's not even dark yet." Jacob stared at her. "Why do you want to leave all of a sudden?"

Liza crossed her arms in a subtly combative gesture. "Because I think leaving right now is a good idea."

"*Good,* Liza...or *sensible*?" There was a trace of cynicism in his response.

"This may come as quite a shock to you, Jacob Van Cleef, but I don't happen to owe you an explanation."

There was an awkward silence. "No," he stated briefly, "I don't suppose you do." He reached into his jacket for the pack of cigarettes. He drew one out and placed it in his mouth, lighting it jerkily. "In fact, you don't owe me anything."

She studied him for a long moment, amazed at the tension in his body. "So now that we've agreed that no explanation is required, are you going to take me home, or should I call a cab?"

The unexpected trace of humor in her question made Jacob raise an eyebrow. "You might have trouble flagging one down, considering it *is* rush hour," he said teasingly. "And, of course, there's the fact that you're two miles from the nearest telephone.... And most important—" he lit his cigarette "—is the particular detail that there's no such thing as a taxicab in Half Moon Falls."

"There's always walking," she declared.

"True, but would you be able to find your way back home in the dark? The sun will be gone pretty soon."

"I'd take my chances."

He gave a hard laugh. "You'd be better off taking your chances with me, Liza."

"I'm not so sure about that." She looked him directly in the eye.

"You enjoyed kissing me," he uttered softly. "Why are you denying it?"

"I'm not denying it," she confessed, "I'm just saying it's time to leave." Deliberately Liza began to gather the remains of the picnic things, replacing them in the straw hamper.

Jacob stilled her arm suddenly. "Did I frighten you tonight?"

"No." In truth, it was her own wild response to this man that had frightened Liza. But there was no way she would ever confess that to anyone, least of all Jacob Van Cleef. Already his enigmatic presence had gained entry into a forbidden zone deep within her. No one, not even Mark, had ever been able to simply reach inside Liza and achieve such a startling intimacy. An intimacy that had nothing at all to do with the physical. It was this strange intimacy that she found most disturbing of all. It went beyond Jacob's sheer sensual power. It intruded in a place where it wasn't welcome.

"I suppose I should apologize," he began in an odd voice.

"Don't apologize. Just take me home now."

"I'll do that," he agreed reluctantly, "but first, you have to do something."

"What?"

"Make me a promise."

She hesitated, still achingly aware of the heat of his fingers on her arm. "Not until I hear what the promise is."

Jacob seemed concerned. "It's this: you'll agree to go out with me again."

"I don't think we should—" Liza began.

"No, wait. *Don't* think, Liza," he urged quietly. "Don't even analyze it. Just say yes."

*Foolish man,* Liza thought later. He hadn't realized there was no question of her refusing another date. For all her protests there was no way she would even consider saying no. This strange relationship that had been launched so precipitously just a few short days ago now had a life of its own. Liza hadn't been trying to refuse Jacob, rather she had been fighting the conflicting demands raging inside herself. She gave a sigh of complete resignation. "Yes. I'll go out with you again."

"Good." Evidently satisfied, he released his hold on her and they continued to gather up the food and utensils. Then both of them stood as they shook out the blanket. Putting the folded blanket across his shoulder, Jacob lifted the basket in one hand, leaving the other one free to guide Liza back up the slippery path.

At one point along the rocky trail, Liza lost her footing and stumbled against Jacob. He steadied her against his hard body, his arm tightly grasping her waist. "Thank you," she said breathlessly.

"You're very welcome." His warm breath fanned the back of her neck, and he held her that way for a long tantalizing moment.

"You can let go now. I've got my balance back."

"It seems I've lost mine," he murmured against her ear. "Liza, what am I going to do with you?"

*Nothing at all, if I have anything to say about it!* Liza cried out silently. But it was a vain hope, she realized. How long could she continue to fight what was so obviously between the two of them? She had come prepared to do battle for a worthy cause, and look how effectively she'd been sidetracked. Tracy and the twins hadn't even come up in the conversation tonight, except that one brief exchange. This evening hadn't turned out at all the way she'd planned; she'd made no inroads in her attempt to help Tracy. Instead she'd done something worse— she'd ended up fraternizing with the enemy.

A reckless journey had begun tonight, and Liza had no way of knowing where it might end. The one thing she *did* know was that dangers lay hidden at every turn on a path more treacherous than the one she now traveled up from the waterfall.

By the time they returned to the truck, the sun had already set behind the horizon, and an eerie dusk lingered heavily over the green hills. In the fading sky a white crescent had not yet begun to glow. The moon hovered dimly, seemingly biding its time, patiently waiting for the darkness of night to fall and become a clean, black backdrop for its bright pearlescence.

Jacob and Liza climbed into the pickup and drove home in virtual silence. It wasn't until much later that Liza realized with regret that she hadn't gotten to see the moon in the water.

# Chapter Six

The first time Liza Langley had been kissed by a
boy she'd been twelve years old. The boy's name was
Valery, and he was the youngest son of the Russian
ambassador, and it had happened at one of the numerous parties that the Washington elite gave during the holiday season.

The adults had believed their children should
practice an innocently youthful brand of "détente."
But the adults were unaware that as soon as the doors
closed, this togetherness translated into rounds of
games popular with adolescents on the verge of
dawning sexuality. Nothing so effectively served the
cause of Soviet-American relations as "Spin the
Bottle" and "Post Office."

It wasn't until her fourteenth birthday that Liza had realized adults conducted negotiations of state in a much more uninteresting way. Well, she thought dryly, that wasn't quite the truth. She hadn't been *that* naive. But it occurred to her that children in general had a far less biased view of the world. Look at Valery Glinka, with his cherubic face and platinum hair. At thirteen he'd giggled and laughed with Liza, dancing happily to the music of Steely Dan and Elton John. Today he was back in Moscow, an active member of the Soviet Press Corps, decrying the decadence of Americans and their culture.

Valery had come up in Liza's thoughts because he reminded her of the twins, somehow. Right now Tommy and Gary were young and free of bias. They could love their older sister and adore Jake at the same time, unable to understand why there was a wedge pressed firmly between them. But sooner or later even the boys would be forced to take sides. Perhaps she was only deluding herself, but Liza believed there was still something she could do to help things.

Surely, there was some way she could help calm the troubled waters. She twisted her lips. All right, the picnic by the waterfall had backfired, if that was what you called it. Still, as long as Liza was going to be around this sleepy little hamlet waiting out her *own* personal thunderstorm, she could keep trying to make herself useful.

Having returned from that date long before Tracy had come home from Fralinglitch, Liza had realized she had a choice. She could keep her evening with Jacob Van Cleef a secret or be open and honest with her friend. She opted for the latter.

"It's not any of my business," Tracy said with a shrug as they sat in the tiny kitchen having coffee. "What you do is your own affair, Liz."

"I know, but the point is—"

"Really—" Tracy gave a weary sigh "—you don't have to explain it to me. I'd be happy if you went out with Donald Duck if it would take your mind off that Mark Sheridan jerk."

"I'm trying to tell you," Liza retorted, "if I can get friendly with Jacob, maybe I could persuade him to ease up on you a little."

"Uh-huh." Tracy rolled her eyes and took another sip from her china mug.

"What's the matter? Don't you think I could do it?"

"Frankly, no."

Liza implored her friend, "Listen, Trace. I feel I'm exceedingly qualified for the job. I'm a disinterested third party, I have a certain degree of experience in the highest levels of diplomacy—"

"Yeah, yeah," Tracy tossed off, "but even your father never came up against anybody like Jake Van Cleef. Trust me."

"I'd still like to give it a shot."

"Take it from one who knows, kid. You'd only be spinning your wheels."

"Fine." Liza paused. "So, do I have your permission to at least *try*?"

"I'm telling you it's a waste of time, Liz. Do you know what a brick wall is?"

"Oh, I know all about brick walls." Liza carried her empty cup over to the sink. "As long as we're on the subject, what are we going to do about you, Miss Tracy MacBride?"

"I haven't the faintest idea what you're talking about."

Liza sighed. "School, Tracy. All those years of struggling to make ends meet. The master's thesis you were near finishing."

"We've already discussed this, Liz. I've put it on the back burner. Believe me, I have every intention of returning to school."

"Really? When?"

Tracy gave an irritated shrug. "Sometime. One of these days... eventually. Oh, how should I know when?"

"How about *never*?" Liza remarked sadly.

"What do you want me to do? Give in to Jake? Hand over my baby brothers and go along my merry way, just because they get in the way of my career?" Tracy's voice rose. "My brilliant, wonderful career that is supposed to be more important than the only little piece of family I have left?"

Seeing Tracy's extreme agitation, Liza realized now, more than ever, that something had to be done to resolve this impossible situation. And soon.

The following morning the worst mistake Liza made was volunteering to drive into the village to pick up the twins from the Bergers' home. It had nothing to do with Mr. and Mrs. Berger, a friendly young couple in their early thirties. Sidney Berger ran Half Moon Falls's only gas station and auto repair shop.

"That Mustang of yours is fantastic. It's in super condition!" he exclaimed with near-reverence. "How many miles does it have on it?"

Rhonda Berger was a sweet-natured, plump woman who smiled a faraway smile at Liza. "It must be so exciting to live in a place like Washington, D.C. All those wonderful goings-on!" She gave an envious sigh. "I love reading those cloak-and-dagger mysteries with all those spies, counterspies and foreign intrigue. Do you get to meet many spies in your neighborhood?"

"Not really." Liza stifled a smile. Actually she knew several people who could be considered "secret agents." They were all unprepossessing individuals who had receding hairlines and wore polyester slacks.

"We were so happy for Tracy when she received that scholarship to the university," Rhonda went on. "How awful that things happened the way they did."

"Yes, isn't it," Liza agreed.

"Of course she had no choice but to face up to her responsibilities." Rhonda paused. "Since she's been home Sidney and I have been racking our brains, trying to find just the right man for her."

"How nice."

"You can just imagine, though, how difficult it is getting a husband for a woman who has a ready-made family, so to speak."

"Absolutely." Liza nodded vaguely and chatted for a few minutes longer before bringing the conversation to a polite but merciful demise. As soon as Sidney Berger removed his head from in front of the odometer, Liza loaded the twins into the car and pulled out of the driveway.

"We had a neat time, Liz!" Gary remarked from behind his comic book. "Joey's got the best refrigerator. Three different flavors of ice bars!"

"My word."

"And malted milk balls! And frozen candy bars!"

Liza grinned. "I'm delighted you've had such a balanced diet." Her words suddenly reminded her that she'd promised Tracy she would stop at the general store for some milk and flour—an action that proceeded to ruin an otherwise pleasant day.

It was one of those pulpy scandal sheets you see so often on grocery checkout stands. Liza was waiting in line with her purchases. The boys kept coming over with packages of goodies they hoped she would add to the basket, like exploding bubble gum and taco-cheese-chips, and Liza found herself unable to refuse any of their requests. A few of the villagers observed her with blunt curiosity. The fact that she was accompanied by two of the town's small but official residents made Liza only *half* a stranger. But she was still an outsider.

Liza smiled at the curious onlookers, and some of them almost smiled back. It probably took them a while to warm up, she thought with amusement. The numerous stares, combined with the repeated solicitations by Tommy and Gary, completely occupied her attention until she moved up to stand right by the counter—and came face to face with the front page of *The National Evening Informer*.

"'His Cheating Broke My Heart!' Cries D.C. Deb," the headline blazed.

Liza felt the bile rise in her throat. She truly thought she would be sick to her stomach right in this rinky-dink little general store. In front of her eyes was a recent picture of Mark and herself at a White House soiree. Fortunately the quality of the photograph was poor, darkening her hair and thickening her facial features until the image scarcely resembled the real Elizabeth Langley. She hoped no one would recognize her, then quickly chided herself. Who in this out-of-the-way town would connect Tracy's friend Liza with the glamorous Elizabeth Langley? Furthermore, who in Half Moon Falls could possibly care?

Certainly Jacob Van Cleef didn't read such gossip tabloids. Even if he'd heard of the Mark Sheridan scandal, if he followed national politics at all, he wouldn't put two and two together. She was Tracy's pal Liz who'd hitchhiked through Europe with her. She was a hostess in an ordinary restaurant, not a rich society woman. No, she continued to work the problem out with reassurance, this wasn't going to cause trouble. Although...Liza glared at the way the newspaper was prominently displayed, and considered possible solutions. Perhaps the only way to make sure her secret would be safe was to buy up all copies of the *Informer*. Suddenly she felt the curious stare of the elderly woman in line behind her.

"Don't you just love that magazine? I find it *so* fascinating."

It was the first complete sentence anyone had said to her since entering the establishment. Liza could only nod weakly and put a single copy in her shopping basket. It would be a major mistake to buy up all the issues, she realized. It would only cause curiosity and engender a great deal of comment...the two things she was hoping so desperately to avoid.

"Can we get baloney loaf?" Tommy asked, intruding on her thoughts.

"How about chocolate-covered pretzel sticks?" Gary brought his latest hopeful addition to the basket.

"Sure, absolutely. Anything you want." Liza couldn't have cared less if they'd asked her to buy out the entire store. Which they almost did.

The law of averages is laden with rules that continually disprove themselves. For example, the tenets that lightning doesn't strike twice, or that if you flip a coin in the air one hundred times it will land on tails half the time. Liza had personally seen a case where lightning struck the same place on two successive days, and actually knew of a situation where a college student had tossed a coin one hundred times, only to have it land on "heads" a total of ninety-nine times. So much for the law of averages. The point was, how much likelihood was there that her car would get a flat tire on the drive home? And what were the odds of Jacob Van Cleef's dusty blue pickup truck being the first vehicle to come along down the road?

Liza had never changed a tire in her life but was attempting to give it a good try. The boys sat contentedly along the grassy shoulder, munching away on food that would have made any ordinary person sick to his stomach. She was just figuring out how to work the jack when the familiar voice inquired, "Need any help?"

She looked up at Jacob's smiling, rugged face and gestured at the uncooperative jack. "What do *you* think?"

"I'm not quite sure. Are you one of those liberated young women who takes any offer of male assistance as a personal insult?"

"It's quite all right. Go ahead and insult me. I'm really having the time of my life trying to lift a two-ton automobile." She paused. "Seriously, Jacob. I'd happily accept any help I can get. I don't have the vaguest idea what I'm doing."

Grinning, he rolled up the sleeves of his denim work shirt and proceeded to raise the car with the jack, deftly remove the bad tire and replace it with a spare. Including tightening the lug nuts, and slipping back on the hubcap, the entire process took less than ten minutes.

"Uncle Jake knows everything there is to know about cars," remarked Gary matter-of-factly.

"Lots more than Mr. Berger, for sure," added Tommy.

"I can see who your biggest fans are," Liza observed.

"Wait until they find out about my feet of clay," came the dry response.

What did Jacob mean by that? Liza decided not to press the issue. Instead, she thanked him for coming by at such an opportune moment. "I really appreciate you fixing that tire for me. Who knows how long I would have stood here like an idiot, trying to figure out how to do it myself." She shrugged helplessly. "I'm not very mechanically inclined."

"Is that a fact?"

"Well, I have been known to change an occasional lightbulb—as long as I have some kind of written instructions."

"We can't all do everything, Liza." He rolled down his sleeves.

"That's true enough. Anyway, thanks again. I'm very grateful."

"Oh, and how grateful is that?"

"What do you mean?"

He leaned his tall frame against the car and studied her face. "Are you grateful enough to have dinner with me tonight?"

The by-now-familiar warning bell sounded. "Well," she hesitated, "I don't really think—"

"That's right." Jacob folded his arms thoughtfully. "Make it a *good* excuse."

"Actually I'm not sure what Tracy has planned."

"Tracy's gonna be at work," Tommy contributed.

"You heard that," Jacob declared. "Tracy has to work."

"Well," Liza murmured, "somebody has to stay with the twins."

"We have a sitter," Gary said, mystified.

"Hey," Liza remembered, "didn't you guys want me to make popcorn with you tonight?"

"We can make popcorn tomorrow," responded Tommy with youthful benevolence.

"All quarters heard from," Jake stated assertively. "You can't get out of it, Liza. You've run out of options."

"Oh, all right," she finally capitulated.

"It won't be *that* bad, I promise you. Why, on some occasions I've even been known to use a knife and fork."

"Yes, I've seen that, if you recall."

"I just thought I'd remind you what a charming dinner companion I can be."

"Is that so?"

"I only bring it up again because some people have exceedingly short memories."

"In case you're wondering," she informed him briskly, "I have a wonderful memory. I can even remember as far back as last night."

Jacob shifted his weight. "That's very interesting. I consider that quite a compliment."

"I didn't mean it to be. I'm just very good when it comes to remembering things."

"Good. I would have hated it if you'd forgotten any minor detail."

"Don't worry. It would take a severe blow to the brain for that, believe me." She tried to sound cynical, but only succeeded in raising Jacob's eyebrows.

There was an odd silence. "I didn't realize I had such a powerful effect on you, Liza."

"I was only kidding," she added quickly.

He shook his head. "Sorry, young lady. It's too late to take the words back. You've already committed yourself." A self-satisfied smile began to spread over his gaunt features.

"What are they talking about?" Tommy nudged his twin.

"Ya got me." Gary rolled his eyes. "Boring adult stuff."

By the time Liza could think of a truly plausible reason to evade Jacob's invitation, he'd already returned to his own vehicle, looking quite pleased with himself. Come to think of it, she decided, her lips twisting at the thought, he'd been insufferably smug about the whole thing. As Liza and the twins got back into the repaired Mustang and continued on their journey homeward, she watched balefully as the blue pickup receded in the rearview mirror.

"Are you going on a date with Uncle Jake?"

Liza nodded tightly. "Kind of. Well, not exactly. Okay, yes, it's a date!"

"Why do grown-ups always kiss on dates?"

Liza felt her face turning red. "They don't always kiss."

"Are you gonna kiss Uncle Jake?"

"You shouldn't ask questions like that."

"How come?"

"Because . . . because they're *embarrassing*, that's why!" She placed a hand on her flushed forehead. Maybe she was coming down with a cold or something.

"I think kissing is yucky!" Tommy declared forcefully. Or was it Gary? At this particular moment, Liza was too flustered to tell one twin from the other.

"If any girl tried to kiss *me*, I'd throw up!" asserted one-half of the twin-spiracy.

"Me, too!" contributed the other half enthusiastically.

"How vivid," Liza muttered, and tried to concentrate on the road. Bless little children and all their endearingly frank observations!

Because she had no idea where Jacob Van Cleef intended to take her for dinner, Liza dressed in a plain pink silk blouse and dark skirt. They were deceptively simple but extremely expensive garments, designed for traveling. They were also the only items of clothing Liza had brought to Half Moon Falls that could even remotely be considered elegant. She'd stuffed the skirt and top into her nylon duffel bag the night she'd fled the house on Foxhall Road. They lay there crushed amongst her T-shirts and sweaters until she'd unpacked them much later. In truth, though, Liza hadn't considered the possibility she would even *need* a skirt and blouse during this self-imposed exile. It only went to prove that her mother's advice was well-founded.

"Even if you travel to a desert island, Liza," her mother had often said, "be sure and take one nice outfit along."

Liza's eyes misted over at the thought of her mother. It was hard to believe it had been nearly six

years since her death. Liza hated to remember her
mother wasting away from the dread disease that had
slowly drained all the strength and vitality from her
beautiful face. Doris Langley had taught her daughter all about being a proper young lady—how to
dress, how to greet guests and how to conduct dinner party conversation. But her mother had died before she could teach Liza certain other things, such
as whether there might be some matters in this world
more important than affairs of state.

She'd never asked her mother if there was something else *she* would rather be doing. And then, of
course, there was the matter of *men*. She wished she
could have asked her mother's advice about men.
What would Doris Langley have thought of Mark
Sheridan? Might she have thought his weakness for
other women a small price for a wife to pay for a
chance at being a First Lady? And what about Jacob Van Cleef? What would Doris Langley have
made of him?

At seven-thirty Jacob arrived at the door, dressed
in a cream pullover and gray slacks. Was it possible,
Liza thought, for a man to grow more attractive with
each successive meeting?

"What are you staring at?" he murmured. "I, at
least, have an excuse." Those strange eyes moved
appreciatively from her head to her toes.

"I was just thinking that you look very nice tonight," Liza stated honestly.

" 'Nice' goes nowhere near describing you, Liza with the golden hair," came his unexpectedly deep reply. His words were so soft and low they might have been a caress.

She forced a light laugh. "Aren't we just the perfect mutual admiration society?"

"Is that what we are?" He studied her intently. "I must admit there's something to be said for being admired—although it's not a position I find myself in very often."

"I find that very hard to believe." It was true that Liza found it more than a little incredible that a man like Jacob Van Cleef had so little personal vanity. What a stunning contrast from her first impression on that country road! For all his bluster and arrogance, he was actually insecure about his appearance, she marveled. On the other hand, this little bit of insecurity did not stop a man from being bossy and tyrannical. And it certainly didn't stop a man from believing he knew everything...including how to read minds!

"This is the first time I've ever seen you in city clothes," he remarked.

"Is that what you'd call these? City clothes?"

"What else would they be?"

"How about a couple of things I tossed in a suitcase?"

"I'll call them anything you like," Jake smiled, "as long as you wear skirts more often. I enjoy seeing your legs, Liza."

She felt heat suffuse her neck, remembering the only other time he had seen her legs. As usual, the man seemed capable of reading her thoughts.

"Or if you prefer, you could wear that bathrobe instead."

Liza decided to ignore the suggestiveness in his tone. "Yes, well. Would you like to see the twins? They're upstairs playing 'Space Invaders.'"

"Changing the subject, are we? Do compliments make you uncomfortable?"

"Only when they're extremely personal."

"And here I thought we'd passed that point, you and I."

"I don't know what 'point' you mean."

"Sure you do, Liza. You know exactly what I'm talking about—" he made a gesture with his hands "—but we don't have to discuss that right now. If you'd prefer to change the subject, I would like to talk to the twins before we go." Jacob glanced over at the babysitter, who was already comfortably ensconced on the sofa with a bag of potato chips, four bottles of nail polish and a television program guide. "Hello, Noreen."

The plump teenager looked up from the television screen just long enough to pop a bubble-gum bubble. "Hi, Mr. Van Cleef," she answered cheerfully. Liza was sure the girl hadn't heard a word of their conversation, and even if Noreen Wilke *had* overheard any of it, she obviously couldn't have cared less. The private social lives of any human beings over the age of twenty was not a subject that elicited her slightest interest. She was fifteen years old, lived next door and was just grateful for the opportunity to make some extra money and have a television set to herself.

Jacob shook his head in resignation. "Wonderful," he murmured under his breath. "I'll go see the twins."

"They'll be delighted to see you."

"And what about you, Liza? Are you delighted to see me, or is this date something you feel forced to suffer under duress?"

"You might be pretty heavy-handed at times, but I seldom do anything I don't want to do," came her even reply.

"I certainly hope that's true." There was a strange note in his voice. "I'd hate to think that any man could make you do something you didn't really want to do."

"Even you?" Liza asked suddenly.

Jacob gazed at her for a long moment. "Especially me." Then almost to himself he repeated the words, "Especially me."

Going upstairs to the boys' bedroom provided a relief from the intensity of their exchange. As usual the place looked as if it had been struck by a cyclone. Although the twins did make their bunk beds every morning, there was nothing else in the room that appeared even remotely neat. Books, toys and games were recklessly strewn everywhere.

"Hi, Uncle Jake," Tommy and Gary said in unison, glancing up from their pile of miniature space cruisers, battle freighters and plastic aliens.

He crossed his arms in exasperation. "This place looks like a war zone."

"It *is* a war zone, Uncle Jake," Tommy said, just as his squadron commander crashed headlong into Gary's battle freighter. "For the past century, the Empire of United Planets has been fighting evil invaders from another galaxy!"

"Yeah!" chimed in Gary, "and we're winning, too!"

Liza shook her head. "You asked for that one, Mr. Van Cleef. As they said, it really is a war zone."

Jacob kneeled down next to the youngsters. "Listen up, you guys. Even war zones have to be neat. How else do you expect to find anything?"

"Aw, we know where all our stuff is!"

"Is that so? Well, I have something else to ask you. Is it fair to make your sister have to clean up after you all the time?" There were thoughtful furrows in his forehead. "She works so hard to take care of you."

"Is that why she cries so much, Uncle Jake?"

Liza thought she actually saw the man flinch. "When does she cry, Gary?" he asked softly.

"Lots of times when she thinks we can't see her."

"Damn," Jacob muttered beneath his breath and glanced at Liza. He drew himself back up to his full height and looked down at the boys from an intimidating distance. "All right, now I'm only going to say this once. Your sister works hard to look after you, and she gets bone-weary. She's on her feet all evening long, which makes her tired during the day. She cleans, she cooks and she's always picking up after you. From now on one place she's not going to pick up after you guys is going to be this room. Understand?"

"But Uncle Jake—"

"No 'buts' about it, Tommy!" He paused. "I'll make you a deal. Keep this room a mess and you won't go to Camp Silverwood this summer. And remember that I said I was going to teach you how to ski this coming Christmas? Keep this room looking like a garbage dump and you can forget that trip, too."

The boys looked contrite. "We'll keep it neat, Uncle Jake."

"Yeah, we promise."

"Very well," he replied loftily, "I'll hold you both to that promise."

Liza was forced to admit that Jacob knew how to handle children firmly yet with affection. As they walked downstairs, he said, "You don't think I was too hard on the kids, do you?"

She had to suppress a smile. "Not at all. In fact, I don't think I've ever seen a man who handles kids as well as you do."

"You really think so?" He seemed pleased.

"Absolutely." Liza wondered if the man had ever thought about having children of his own, but decided that such a question would be far too personal.

For dinner, they drove to a new restaurant that had just opened along the route to Silverwood Lake, offering the only competition to the Fralinglitch Inn for miles around. "I know you must be wondering why I'm not taking you to the restaurant where Tracy works."

"A little," she admitted. *Of course, she wondered why.* Did Tracy make him so uncomfortable that he would go out of his way to avoid her? Somehow Jacob didn't seem like a man who could be intimidated by anybody.

"I know the Fralinglitch Inn is the leading restaurant in the county. It's been there since the revolutionary war—George Washington himself slept there."

"He certainly got around, that George."

"Well, the point is, it seems I've been eating at the inn my entire life. I know everybody who goes there and everybody knows me." Jake turned his eyes from the road for a brief instant. "Frankly, I was thinking of having a quiet evening away from prying eyes."

"I understand completely," Liza said, then almost wished she hadn't. She didn't mean to imply that she was looking forward to being alone with Jacob Van Cleef. What she meant was that as Elizabeth Langley she could rarely patronize her favorite Washington restaurants without being fawned over by people who knew her from the social circuit. Sometimes it wasn't such a bad thing seeing people she knew, but in the past year, during her engagement to Mark, there had been lightbulbs flashing everywhere they went. How very well Liza understood Jacob's remark. She'd been up against "prying eyes" her entire life. Of course, there was no way to let the man sitting alongside her in the pickup know anything about it.

"I was hoping you'd feel that way," came the soft reply. The warmth of his smile radiated through the cab.

The restaurant was Nicole's, a tiny oasis of French cuisine in what Jacob admitted was a barren culinary desert. It was housed in a converted barn made charming by the owner's collection of antiques and memorabilia from her native Normandy. Nicole, a thin and regal woman in her early sixties, did all the cooking. The serving was done by her husband, Paul, a dour-faced man she had met during his service with the U.S. Army during World War II. After retiring from his job at the post office he had supported his wife's lifelong dream of running her own restaurant. If this evening's meal was any indication, Nicole's could only be an unqualified success.

"This *cassoulet* is magnificent," Liza told Jacob enthusiastically. She didn't tell him that the last time she had tasted such a superb version of the classic goose, sausage and white bean dish had been at a dinner for the French premier.

All Jacob knew was that Liza was enjoying herself immensely, and his choice of restaurants had been an unqualified success. He watched her animated face from across the small table. It was amazing to see the way her blue-gray eyes seemed to gleam back at him in the flickering candlelight. "I'm glad you like it," he murmured, taking another sip of Bordeaux. He was thirty-six years old, too old to be having romantic fantasies, or so he thought. For the past ten years, the heavy burden of responsibilities had made Jacob feel as if he were at least twenty years older.

He didn't carry just his own burdens; he carried the weight of his father's indiscretions and tortured secrets. He had never truly liked his father, and when the man had died seven years ago, he'd left behind the wreckage of other lives shattered by his cruelty and thoughtlessness. Good people, kind creatures, like his own mother—and even Tracy MacBride, the poor girl who at one time had looked up to Jake as a friend, only to feel so betrayed and astonished later in that sorry affair with his brother, Peter. He'd had to go along with his father's wishes and break the young couple up—God knows, there had been no choice on *that* score.

Jake had learned to live with Peter's bitterness and Tracy's hurt, knowing she could never understand because she would never know the painful reasons behind Jake's actions. He'd spent the years trying to find ways to make it up to her, but Tracy would always hate him, that much was clear. There would never be a way to set things straight, and he'd finally accepted it, although it hadn't been easy. He was always aware of his father's secret sins hanging over him like a dark, oppressive cloud.

Then, unexpectedly, he'd met Tracy's friend Liza. Standing on a country road, they'd raged back and forth at each other that fateful Saturday dawn. But inside, he'd been elated. He'd felt like singing that song "Angel in Blue Jeans." Maybe he was going nuts or something, but what a delightful sensation after all these years of emptiness. Watching Liza now, Jacob felt an odd contentment. Was this what "happy" was supposed to feel like? Happiness had become such an alien emotion, he was no longer sure.

Jake realized he'd never wanted anything or anyone as much as he wanted Liza right now. The only barrier between them was her loyalty to Tracy. Jake cursed his father again. If only—but, no, he couldn't change the past. He gritted his teeth. All he could do was try to break that barrier down and exert complete control over the present. He would tear down that wall of distrust and scatter those tiny seeds of doubt. Once again, Jake smiled at his lovely dinner companion. "Would you care for some more Bordeaux?"

Liza nodded and held out her wine goblet. "Thank you, Jacob."

*Jacob.* He poured the wine, still feeling the thrill of hearing his given name on her lips. No one had ever called him Jacob with that same breathy quality. Okay, he told himself for the hundredth time as he refilled his own glass, maybe he *was* getting a bit carried away. Liza was a delicious and lovely creature, but she was no angel. There were obviously some items in her past that she was attempting to conceal from him. Apparently she'd been the instigator behind Tracy and Liza's wild times in Europe. Lord only knew the type of life Liza led in Washington these days.

But who was he to judge? Jake admitted. It would be somewhat hypocritical, considering all the wild oats he'd sown in his younger years. Besides, when an attraction for someone was this strong, a man could afford to overlook a few flaws. Jacob certainly wasn't going to complain because the woman wasn't as pure as the driven snow, just waiting for the right man to come along. And he also had no intention of turning into some sentimental idiot the way some men did as they drew close to forty.

An enchanting little creature could come along, Jacob knew, and the next thing a man knew, he was wrapped around her finger—not caring what the reality of the situation was, but wanting only to savor the exquisite illusion. Jacob Van Cleef looked up from his wineglass into the bright silver-blue gaze across the table and received another jolt to his senses. Perhaps reality wasn't terribly important right now, he thought suddenly. Maybe being an idiot sometimes had a great deal to recommend it. In fact, it might not be such a bad idea at all. He could even grow to like it. . . .

After coffee and a delectable apple pastry for dessert, they started homeward. Jacob had every intention of driving Liza directly home. Or so he told himself. But things didn't work out that way.

Liza found Jacob's strange silences during dinner and now along the trip home both baffling and disturbing. She had been so sure, at first, that he'd been having as pleasant a time as she was. But she was beginning to wonder if maybe the man had found her boring. Perhaps he had other things on his mind. Well, she decided, *it's now or never.* Tonight had to be the proper time to bring up the subject of Tracy and the twins. She cleared her throat. "Jacob," she began tentatively, "I realize it's probably none of my business, but there's something I must discuss with you."

"What is it?"

"Uh, well, I'm not sure how else to put this, so I'll get right to the point—"

"Sounds pretty serious, Liza," he said lightly.

Oh, *great*, she groaned inwardly, this is the last thing he's going to want to talk about. In fact, he'll most likely be annoyed. But she forced herself to brazen it out. "It is pretty serious. It's about Tracy."

The temperature in the cab instantly dropped by at least fifteen degrees. "I see," an icy voice answered. "So that's what this is all about."

"I realize it isn't my place, but—"

"You're right, it isn't," he said, cutting her off abruptly.

"I realize you want what's best for the boys, but—" Liza decided to forge ahead, anyhow. It was what Arthur himself would have done in similar circumstances. No, that wasn't quite true. Ambassador Arthur Langley had probably never been alone with a devastatingly attractive man on a lonely country road at night. And even if he *had* been, it just wasn't the same thing, Liza thought, twisting her mouth ironically.

Jacob uttered an inaudible oath and pulled the truck over to the side of the road, abruptly shutting off the ignition. "All right, since you're so hell-bent on opening this can of worms, let's *talk* about it, then!"

Liza was starting to wonder if she'd pushed the man too far. She was torn with feelings of disloyalty. Part of her wanted to set things straight for Tracy's sake, and another part of her didn't want to talk about anything but the moonlight and waterfalls. She must be out of her mind. Again, Liza cleared her throat. "As I was saying, I realize you want what's best for the twins—"

Jacob stared back at her with hooded eyes. "I also want what's best for Tracy."

"Sure, I understand that, too, but—"

"No," Jacob said quietly. "You don't understand at all. You don't understand anything about it."

"I know enough to see that Tracy is terrified of being shut out."

"What are you talking about?"

Liza crossed her arms. "If things had been different, I truly believe Tracy might have willingly entrusted the boys to your care. But because of what happened all those years ago, she doesn't believe you can be trusted to share the twins."

"You think I don't know that?" he responded angrily. "You think I don't know she hates me because of Peter?"

Liza studied his tense face. "I have to know, Jacob. Why? Why did you do it?"

"I won't discuss that. Not ever."

"Tracy loved your brother."

"She got over it," came the clipped reply.

"I've heard of people being snobs, but could you have been that ashamed of Tracy dating your—"

"Liza." She had never heard a tone so hard, like cold steel. "Listen to me," Jacob uttered. "If I could change the past, I would. If I could alter the way I behaved back then, I would. I might have handled things differently, but I didn't. It's all spilled milk now."

"But why did you do it at all? It makes no sense that someone like you would do something so cruel and unfeeling—"

"Let's just say I'm my father's son," Jacob said in a rusted tone. "He had a way of making people do things. I had no choice but to do what he wanted."

"What do you mean, you had no choice?"

"I don't care to discuss this, Liza. There's no useful purpose to be served in dredging up the past."

Liza sensed something else in his voice. A kind of raw regret. It was so completely unexpected that she didn't know what to make of it. Impulsively she reached out and touched Jacob's hand. He flinched as if he'd been stung. "Listen to me," she said in a kinder tone, "I still believe it's possible to make peace with Tracy."

"I wish I shared your confidence."

"The first step is obvious."

"Oh?"

"If you really want to improve the situation, I suggest you put off any plans to sue Tracy for custody of the twins."

"They'd be far better off with me. Besides, Tracy doesn't belong here as a nursemaid. She should be back in school, getting her master's degree." Jacob argued angrily.

"I agree."

He looked at her in surprise. "You agree with me?"

"Of course I do. You forget I was there with Tracy the past five years. I watched her struggle. Even with that scholarship she didn't have enough to make ends meet."

"I realize it wasn't enough, but any more money and she might have gotten suspicious," Jacob said quietly.

"What do you mean she might have gotten suspicious?" Liza stopped suddenly. "You?" She stared in amazement. "You're the one who gave Tracy that scholarship?"

Jacob seemed embarrassed. "Listen to me, Liza. She has no idea, and she must never know, is that clear?"

"But why—"

"I wanted Tracy to have a chance, a chance at being everything she wanted to be. So much of her unhappiness is my family's fault. I thought if she could get away from this town she always hated—"

"But Jacob, don't you see? If Tracy knew that you were the one who helped her, she might change her—"

"No, it wouldn't change a thing." He sighed, "Please, I don't want to talk about it anymore."

Liza relented. "All right, then. What *would* you like to talk about?"

Jacob didn't say anything for a moment, then suddenly he leaned across the seat and pulled Liza into his arms. "How about *you*, Liza?"

She gave a convulsive swallow. "Me?"

"It's a subject I've been thinking about all evening. I think it's time we discussed it." His fingers brushed gently across the delicate line of her jaw.

Liza struggled to free herself from his dizzying closeness. "Frankly, I don't have a great deal to say about that particular subject."

"Oh, but I do," he gave a cryptic smile, "I find the subject of Liza infinitely fascinating. Shall I show you more specifically?" In another instant, Jacob silenced her protests with a searing kiss that left her senses reeling. Her mouth parted against the insistent probing of his hard tongue as he drank in the moist sweetness waiting within, then continued to search for new plunder. He nibbled the tender lobe of her ear and caressed the smooth skin of her nape with the tips of his fingers. Liza gave a moan of pleasure.

"Do you like it when I touch you like this?" he uttered hoarsely. "Should I touch you some more, honey?" he repeated against the sensitive column of her throat.

"Yes, Jacob!"

"God, I love it when you say my name like that," he rasped. "Say it again!"

"Jacob."

"Now tell me what you want me to do," he urged against her ear.

"Touch me, Jacob."

"God, yes!" His own voice unsteady, Jacob greedily returned to the heated moistness of her mouth. He was burning his brand deep into the core of her.

To Liza, this was an exotic new world of sensation. She didn't understand it. She didn't want to understand it. She was on sensory overload, and all she wanted to do was *feel*.

"Oh, woman, how you delight me," he murmured against the silk of her nape. "Don't stop!"

"Stop what?" Liza asked huskily, then realized she'd been running her fingers through his hair in a totally unconscious gesture. It was dark and smooth. How nice, she thought, to be so completely aware of a man this way.

"Keep touching me, honey." Jake's eyes shut convulsively. "I want you to touch me," he begged yet demanded in the same breath.

Liza continued to explore and caress with delicious freedom. She planted tentative kisses across his forehead, his roughened cheeks and along the strong line of his jaw. Liza had never had the least inclination to take the initiative with any of the other men she'd known. Yet here she was, with a man who was still a stranger to her in so many ways, a man she had only known for a handful of days, and all she wanted to do was shower one gentle caress after another upon him. "Is *this* the way you want me to touch you?" Liza whispered against the tensed cord of his throat.

"Yes." His voice came out a rasp.

"And this way?" She brushed delicate butterfly kisses across his ear.

"Sweet torture," he moaned approvingly, then at once took his own initiative again. Wrapping his strong arms around her, he pressed Liza down against the soft leather of the seat, imprinting her body with his masculine hardness. As his lips burned a trail of liquid fire down the base of her neck, deft fingers began to unfasten the top buttons of her silk blouse. Now his hands and lips headed toward the shadowy cleft between her breasts. And now those same little warning bells from the evening before began to ring again.

Up until that moment Liza had been lost, utterly lost in the wild, sensual abandon of Jacob's kisses. Now, the reality of where this could be heading reached Liza with the shock of new awareness. As his hard fingers unbuttoned the next button and reached to caress one firm, small breast, the warning bells grew louder.

"Jacob, wait!" She stilled his insistent hand.

"What?" came his hoarse response.

"Listen to me—" Liza searched for the right words "—everything is happening too fast!"

He stared down at her, his eyes dark with passion. "Do you know what you're doing to me? Do you have any idea?"

"This is starting to get out of control," she protested breathlessly.

"No, honey," he countered huskily, "it's been out of control for a long, long time." With that he pressed her more tightly against him, making her even more aware of the intensity of his desire. His hard, muscled thighs moved urgently in rough rhythm to the rising storm.

"Please!"

"Please what, love?" He pulled the blouse away from one shoulder and kissed the bare, satiny skin.

"Stop. We must stop now!" she whispered the plea against the spicy scent of his hair.

"But what if I don't want to stop?"

"It *must*, Jacob," she announced firmly. "It must stop this minute!"

Somehow the warning tone in her voice finally got through to him. With a strangled oath, Jacob lifted his head at last and, in a reluctant motion, freed her from his heavy grasp. Obviously with great effort, still breathing raggedly, he drew himself up to a sitting position.

As soon as they pulled apart Liza felt a flush of shame. How could she have lost herself this way? How could she have been driven into such a frenzy? It especially disturbed her because she'd sometimes been accused of being cold. She'd turned stiffly away from crude kisses, almost accepting the coldness as her own inability to feel. Even Mark, in a moment of extreme frustration, had referred to her as "the ice queen." But just look what might have happened inside the cab of this pickup truck alongside a nameless country road. With a man she hadn't even known for a week! Feelings of embarrassment quickly extinguished any remaining sparks of passion.

"Are you all right?" Jacob spoke for the first time since pulling back from that heated embrace.

"Fine," Liza just wanted to be ten thousand miles away from here.

"Damn," he muttered harshly, and cupped her chin in one hand. "I can't take much more of this, Liza."

"I'm sorry—"

"Don't be sorry, just let me have you." He reclaimed her lips with a new urgency, an urgency laced with fear. "Don't pull away from me again."

"Please!" With an effort, she turned her face away from the renewed demands of his mouth. "Can't you understand that I really want you to stop, Jake?"

For the first time, he seemed to finally hear her pleas. He sighed harshly. "I suppose you didn't like what I was doing."

"I *did* like it."

A muscle in his jaw tightened. "Then why did you make me stop?"

"Because in another moment I wouldn't have wanted you to."

"Damn right," he practically growled. "Why do you play these teasing games with me, Liza?"

"Teasing games?" she practically choked. "If that's what you can say after what just happened, then you're the densest man I've ever met!"

"You must know some interesting men."

"That's more true than you'll ever realize, Mr. Jacob 'Holier-Than-Thou' Van Cleef. I know men whose accomplishments can only be called legendary!"

"If you know what's good for you, you won't mention other men right now," he threatened darkly.

"I'll do as I please." Liza narrowed her eyes. "What right do you have to use that ominous tone with me?"

"I have every right," Jacob ground out.

"Oh, this is fascinating! What gives you the so-called right to threaten me like this?"

"I've had the right since you almost ran me off the road last Saturday."

"Oh, is *that* what this is all about? You still think I'm to blame for that stupid curve in the road?"

"I don't care about that stupid curve in the road, Liza. I'm trying to explain to you why I've had the right ever since I met you," Jacob said with disturbing calm. "The right to touch you. The right to hold you and kiss you. The right to make love with you."

Liza trembled involuntarily at the ache in his words. "You have no rights over me," she said in a low voice. "I am my own person."

"How can you say that, Liza, when you know very well you belong to me?"

"I *what*?" Her eyes widened.

"Do you find that so shocking?"

Liza felt the need to gasp for air. Was it possible that this man was actually saying what she thought he was saying? Or were her ears playing tricks on her? Perhaps it was the aftereffect of too much Bordeaux.

"I asked you a question," he said tautly.

"I'm still trying to come up with an answer." She must be going mad, Liza decided. Things like this simply didn't happen to Elizabeth Langley of the Foxhall Road Langleys. Men didn't lose their heads over her and claim her with such raw, old-fashioned machismo. She was a political asset and an ice queen. How could Jacob Van Cleef talk to her this way, his eyes and voice dark with unassuaged hunger?

"I guess you are shocked." There was genuine astonishment in his statement.

"No one ever said what you just said to me," she confessed simply. "It takes a minute to assimilate a remark like that."

"Well, I've never said it to anyone before." There was a note of cool irony in his reply.

"I find that very hard to believe."

"Why?"

"Because you seem so...so *experienced* in these matters."

He reached over to the dashboard and drew out a cigarette. "Physically I've got plenty of experience—" there was a significant pause "—but then, don't we all?'' Through her confusion Liza wondered what he meant. "I'm talking about the emotions, Liza," Jacob continued as she tried to sort out her racing thoughts. "I don't have a lot of experience when it comes to them. If I said something outrageous and stupid just now, I'm sorry. This is all a little new to me."

"Oh." For the first time the extent of his vulnerability was painfully obvious. Liza was stunned at his willingness to be so open. She wished she had the courage to be the same.

Already, though, it was too late. The hard, brick wall had begun building up again around the enigmatic man. "If I did anything to frighten you, I'm sorry."

"You didn't frighten me."

"What did I do then?"

"I already told you that. You went too fast, Jacob. You want everything at once, and I can't give it. I don't think I'm ... ready," she said with a regretful sigh.

"What would it take for you to be ready?" he asked darkly.

She evaded his eyes. "Please, Jacob. I won't be rushed like this. It's too confusing. I need more time."

"All you need is time?" he echoed sharply, "Do you expect me to really believe that?"

"Yes. Why would I lie to you, of all people?"

"I don't know. I must be crazy. I've never been out of control like this before. I've never said things like that to anyone." He struck a match savagely. "Let's forget I ever said anything at all!"

"But Jacob, wait—"

"Let's just drop it, Liza, and chalk the whole thing up to a lousy bottle of Bordeaux!" Thrusting the truck into gear, he headed home.

# Chapter Seven

He was a fool, thought Jacob Van Cleef. He was a complete, unadulterated idiot. Over and over again he replayed the evening in his mind—the entire debacle of the night before. He'd kissed and touched Liza until he knew the fire in her matched his own raging demands. Or at least, so he'd thought. When he'd opened himself up to her and revealed his raw need—something he'd never done in his entire life— her response had been not pleasure but anger.

"Damn!" He muttered to himself again. How could he have misjudged a woman the way he had misjudged Liza? Getting all poetic. Thinking of meadows in the springtime and angels in blue jeans? Come on! He must have been completely off his rocker!

Oh, he still wanted her, that much was true. And he certainly had no intention of giving her up. If she actually thought she was going to return to Washington, D.C., any time in the near future, she had a few surprises coming. That was clear enough, but Jacob had learned his lesson. He would never leave himself open to emotional damage again. He desired Liza, and he intended to have her, but it would stay just where it should remain...as a physical obsession. No romantic delusions. No flights of fancy.

In his outrage, it only briefly occurred to Jacob that Liza's hot-cold response last night could have been due to inexperience. That possibly only a woman who had never completely been with a man could have failed to receive his erotic message. Only a woman incredibly naive and virginal could have had feelings, genuine feelings that matched his own, but been afraid to act on them. But the concept of Liza's being a virgin barely hovered in his consciousness for an instant before Jake dismissed it as a wishful fairy tale.

Liza was a bohemian who had carelessly traveled the highways of Europe in her jeans and knapsack. She had hitchhiked in France and Spain with careless hippie abandon. She lived a dubious life in Washington and claimed to be some kind of hostess in a restaurant—most probably a cocktail lounge at best. He could just imagine her in the shortest, tightest, skimpiest of serving costumes—and that was a mistake. For all her flaws, it only made him want her more. But this time he would be careful, Jake promised himself. Whatever happened between them would have to be on his terms—terms that he would make beneficial to them both. She wouldn't be able to turn him down. He'd make it well worth her while. But somehow the laugh of triumph he uttered at the thought came out strangely hollow.

"Well, what on earth is the matter with you this morning?" Tracy asked her friend.

Liza was hunched over the kitchen table, still in her bathrobe, dark shadows under her eyes. "Nothing."

"Oh, I'm *sure*!"

"Really, it's nothing."

"Have you been crying?" her friend asked, eyeing her suspiciously.

"Certainly not! What on earth gave you such a stupid idea?" But Liza knew her voice had risen a little too high and a trifle too quickly to make her words convincing.

"Was it something Jake did?"

There was a pause. "Why would you think this has anything to do with him?" came the brittle reply.

"Then something is wrong. You admit it." Tracy shook her head. "Boy, Liz, do I know *you* well!"

"I don't want to talk about it."

"What did he do?"

"I already told you, I'm not discussing this with you, Trace."

"Why not? Aren't friends supposed to share everything, especially confidences?"

"Take a hint, all right?" Liza pleaded.

Tracy sighed good-naturedly. "Okay, okay. I'll leave it alone for now."

"Thank you so *very* much," Liza replied sarcastically.

"But I take it this means you're completely over Mark Sheridan?"

"You do have a point." Liza considered Tracy's astute observation for a moment. "However, if it's quite all right with you, I'd prefer to howl at the moon by myself right now."

"A lot you know. It's ten o'clock in the morning. There's no moon." Tracy was mystified.

"I was speaking metaphorically."

"I haven't the vaguest idea what you're talking about, Liz, but I will take a hike."

"Is that a promise?"

"Damn it, Liz!" Tracy gave an impatient pout and plopped down into one of the chrome and vinyl chairs. "I'm your friend. Don't you want to talk to me?"

Liza gave a resigned sigh. "I don't know if you're ready to hear this."

"Sure I am. Don't you know I'm always ready for anything?" Her friend grinned. "With brothers like Tommy and Gary around, you've *got* to be!"

"Considering the situation, you might not like what I'm about to tell you," Liza was tentative.

"I never said I would like it, only that I wanted to hear about it. So shoot!"

Liza didn't know where to begin. "Up until two weeks ago, I thought I was in love with Mark."

"A major aberration," Tracy remarked. "So what's the problem?"

"Now, two weeks later…is it possible that I could be—"

"Uh-oh, hold on a second, I think I know what's coming!"

"In love with another man?"

"No. Not Jacob Van Cleef." Tracy shook her head in consternation. "Not out of all the men you might have rebounded to."

Maybe Tracy was right, Liza thought for a moment. Maybe she was rebounding. But in Liza's heart she knew it wasn't true. She was starting to fall in love with Jacob. Last night her feelings had been too new, too shocking to fully comprehend. The concept of loving another man so quickly after the debacle with Mark seemed incomprehensible. What did that say about the depths of her feelings for her former fiancé? How could she be so fickle? Then again, if she had been deluding herself all along and never truly been in love with Mark, how could she ever trust her feelings again?

Then Liza realized something. She honestly didn't care. It simply didn't matter. Whatever she felt for

Jacob Van Cleef was inexplicable, but it was strong and true. She was through with always analyzing things.

"Not Jake, of all people," Tracy groaned irritably again.

"I told you that you weren't going to like it."

"Gosh, are you sure, Liz?"

"Yes, unfortunately," she confessed. The problem was going to be getting the man to talk to her again after last night's misunderstanding. She'd just have to sit him down and make him listen. As far as the physical thing was concerned, she'd explain everything to him so that Jacob really understood she hadn't been leading him on. Even though this was the first time in her twenty-four years she had ever felt that indescribable magic with anyone, she had been afraid to follow it through. As a virgin, the awesome power of her own passion for Jacob had frightened her. Had he taken things more slowly and taken the time to guide her, Liza would have followed his lead, and gladly.

"So what are you going to do about it?" Tracy's words fell on deaf ears.

Liza was already lost in her own thoughts. Bitterly, she recalled her own abortive attempts at intimacy with Mark. It had all seemed so awkward, so artificial, that nothing had ended up happening. Liza had been convinced that marriage would change her feelings of coldness and had decided to wait until the wedding night. But now she realized it had nothing to do with marriage. Or at least the actual state of matrimony. It had to do with love. Sometimes in this world a person had to take a chance, Liza reasoned. And this time was as good as any. She would take her chances with Jacob Van Cleef—big and stubborn, somewhat rough around the edges... She was willing to take the risk.

For some reason Jacob wasn't surprised to receive a phone call from Liza. He was sitting in his office at the Van Cleef Dairy thinking about her, so when the phone suddenly rang and his secretary told him who the caller was, he was impressed by the absolute justice—the poetic justice—of the situation.

"I hope you don't mind my calling you at work, Jacob." Her voice actually sounded shy, if that could be believed.

"Oh, I don't mind at all." Jacob was proud of how incredibly casual he sounded.

"I was wondering if—" Liza hesitated.

"If what?"

"Do you think we could get together when you have some time?"

"I suppose that could be arranged." How cool his reply was, Jacob congratulated himself.

"It's just that..." Liza was suddenly at a loss for words. After all, she reasoned, how did one arrange a meeting to tell a man you might be in love with him? With all her vast knowledge of etiquette and experience in protocol, this was one predicament in which she showed an appalling lack of expertise.

"It's just that *what*, Liza?" Jacob tried not to sound overly smug. It was obvious she'd had second thoughts about her behavior last night and now wanted to offer the traditional olive branch. Fine. He would show her just how forgiving and magnanimous he could be.

"Oh, I'll tell you when I see you," Liza said, suddenly shy all over again.

Jake agreed to see her at lunchtime in his office. He had decided to keep the setting as official and businesslike as possible. Not that he ever doubted for a minute who would be the person in control.

Several hours later, dressed in jeans and a knit shirt, Liza drove to the Van Cleef Dairy. The managing offices were in a two-story wood frame building with a white picket fence, set in the same pasture as the buildings that housed the gentle Holsteins themselves.

A polite but brusque older woman, obviously Jacob's secretary, ushered Liza into the office. It was a paneled room, with burnished leather armchairs and rich wood furniture. It was all antique, and Liza, who could recognize fine old wood, could appreciate the way it had mellowed. The office resembled Arthur Langley's study in the house on Foxhall Road, but Liza had trouble noticing anything in the room except the man who sat silently at the desk before her.

Jacob was reading a newspaper when she entered the room, and he continued to look at it for a moment before putting it down in front of him. Unfortunately Liza had time to read one of the lead news headings—"Chief Envoy's Hopes High for Summit." There was no way she could fight it, thought Liza. Her father and her life in Washington would always be with her.

"Hello, Liza." Jacob was excruciatingly polite. "Are you interested in current events?"

"Not particularly."

"You seem to be staring at my newspaper with undisguised fascination."

What was he going on about? She was here to talk about her feelings, not current events! "As I already said, I don't find current events especially exciting."

"Oh, but I do. There are wonderful things like heart transplants and peace talks. Here's another article about the godfather of modern diplomacy, the great Arthur Langley himself. That man must be seventy if he's a day, and still going strong."

*Actually he's seventy-three,* Liza said silently. "I didn't think you were impressed with politics, Jacob." Okay, she'd talk about anything but the subject on her mind...anything that would help her get over her nervousness.

"I'm not, but I've always found Langley a fascinating figure. One of the few people in the government that I happen to admire."

"I'm sure he'd be delighted to hear it. You must be sure to tell him that when you meet him." Liza spoke without thinking.

Jacob thought she was being sarcastic and played along. "I know this will come as somewhat of a shock to you, Liza, but Arthur Langley and I don't happen to move in the same social circles."

*Do you want to bet?* Liza gave a weak smile. "Look, Jacob—" it was now or never "—I wanted to talk to you about what happened or, to be precise, *didn't* happen, last night."

A muscle tensed in Jacob's jaw. "Go ahead. I'm all ears." The mood inside the office changed abruptly.

It was exceedingly awkward to talk about what Liza wanted to talk about when the subject of her discourse sat stiffly behind his desk, treating her as if this were some kind of business meeting or job interview. She realized he was probably still hurt and confused, but this was maddening! "The point is," she continued, "that I want you to know, Jacob, that—" There was another awkward pause. It was one thing to *feel* something, but another to openly express that feeling in words. He just sat behind that desk of his, not saying a word. Damn, he was making it very difficult, wasn't he? "I want you to know—" Liza began again.

He sat there coolly. "Is there some sort of problem? What exactly are you trying to say?"

"Please, Jacob, this isn't very easy for me."

For a moment, Jake's eyebrow raised at the strange note of vulnerability in Liza's voice. Then he decided it must be his imagination. *Wishful thinking.* "Say what you came here to say," he uttered harshly. "I've got quite a bit of work to do."

Why was he being so unbelievably hard? Was his male ego so deflated from the evening before? Maybe she shouldn't have come here at all. There was a limit to how much anyone, no matter what she felt for him, could be permitted to bully her. "Well, then," she retorted, "if you're so terribly busy, then what I have to say can't be that important. Perhaps we should just forget it."

"Liza, wait." Jacob came from around the desk.

"I'll just come back another time when it's more convenient. Then again, maybe I just won't come back at all." She turned on her heels to leave, feeling incredibly hurt.

"Liza." He caught up behind her, wrapping his arms around her waist. "I'm a jerk. I don't know what I'm doing." He buried his mouth in her hair. "Go ahead, baby. Tell me what you came here to say."

Liza gave a sigh. "I care about you, Jacob. I wanted you to know that I care about you very much." That was a start. It would take a few moments to build up to the "love" part. Now she waited for his response.

"I've been waiting to hear you say that, Liza." That was all he said.

"About wanting to make love to me last night—" she began shyly, then stopped.

"Are you trying to say that you've changed your mind about that, too?" Jacob inquired smoothly. Yes, it was going so predictably. The woman was so transparent!

"I think so." Liza paused with embarrassment. "If we took things slowly, it would be very nice to make love with you, Jacob." *Nice* was such an awful word, but this conversation was so awkward as it was! Wasn't it about time Jake helped her out? Why was he acting so glib and aloof?

"So, you think it would be nice to make love with me, Liza?" he echoed slowly, turning her around in his arms. She could feel the warmth of his chest through his shirt and smell the spicy aroma of his after-shave. Lowering his face so that his mouth hovered scant inches above hers, he murmured, "Why am I wasting my time talking, when I should be kissing the breath out of you? Come here, honey!" His warm breath mixed with hers as he lowered his lips to claim her waiting mouth.

# Chapter Eight

As Jake's lips lingered on Liza's in a magical, electrifying kiss, his hands traveled down past her waist to mold her hips to his.

Liza was thrilled to lose herself in the enchantment all over again. She reached up and wrapped her arms around his neck, pressing her slim body even more intimately against his. How could she ever have doubted her feelings for this man? He was everything, in a hundred ways, that Mark Sheridan could never be. There was a harsh side to him, but it was balanced by a tender side. Why couldn't she have accepted the raw honesty of his emotions last night? Why had it frightened her instead of exciting her the way she was aroused right at this moment? Jacob's kisses grew more demanding, and Liza responded in

kind—opening her mouth once more to his exquisite probing.

"Yes, that's it," he urged approvingly. "Why did
you keep me waiting last night, Liza?"

"I don't know why," she gasped between hungry
kisses. Truly, she couldn't imagine what had possessed her last night. Why had she run away from
such a delicious promise of fulfillment? But none of
that mattered now. Nothing mattered but Jacob
continuing to hold her against his male hardness,
pulling her own warmth into his. "Just keep touching me, Jacob!"

"I will, honey." His voice thickened with passion. "Nothing will make me stop now. You can bet
on that!" Deft hands moved along the waistband of
her jeans, freeing her T-shirt from the constraining
belt. Once they had gained entry to the warm flesh of
her stomach, Jacob's determined hands continued to
travel upward until they reached the silky lace cov-
ering her small, firm breasts.

"What are you doing?" she breathed.

"I'm undressing you, darling," came the thick
reply. For a moment he cupped her breasts in his
hands, the burning heat of his touch immediately
imprinting itself through the flimsy material of her
bra. In a moment he had discovered the front clasp
that confined her breasts and unhooked it. The cool
air whispered against Liza's bare skin as both the
scrap of lingerie and her T-shirt were skillfully drawn
away. "You're so beautiful!" Jacob exclaimed in a

rough voice, lowering his mouth to one of the pink-tipped peaks. "So perfect!" His tongue savored the satin skin, teasing the nipple to hardness.

What was happening? Liza's senses screamed at the exquisite pleasure of his expert caresses. She was losing herself in an erotic whirlpool, spinning deeper and deeper, out of control. And she didn't care. It was all right to lose control. It was the right thing to do because this was the right man at last. This was the man who would show her how to ride the maelstrom. Hard fingers brushed tauntingly back and forth across the tender orbs while Jacob's roving mouth sought out the taut silk of her stomach. His hot tongue drew circles against her own aching flesh, and then the hands returned to the waistband of her jeans, this time unsnapping them to reach the thin scrap of matching pink panties.

"Jacob, please!" she heard a shocked gasp she recognized as her own plea for something, but even now, burning as she was with the fever for fulfillment, Liza dared not acknowledge it with the words.

"What do you want?" Jacob rasped with increasing urgency. "Tell me what you want, darling!"

"I . . . I want you," she pleaded, "I want *you*, Jacob."

His skillful hands unzipped the jeans completely and began to pull them down Liza's slender thighs. "Do you know how long I've been waiting for you to say that?" He drew a deep breath and put her away from him firmly. "Let me just go and lock the door, honey. I don't want anyone to disturb us." He planted a hard kiss of total possession at the sensitive base of her throat. In just a few quick strides he reached the door of his office and returned almost immediately, enfolding her in his muscular strength and lifting her up in his arms.

"Jacob, what...what are we—" Liza was at once shocked and tantalized by the prospect of what was about to happen. She was being carried in this wonderful man's arms, the male scent of him brushing against her face where it lay pressed to his chest. He smelled of soap, after-shave and crisp, clean cotton. He was going to carry her to the long, soft leather couch and make love to her in his office in the middle of the day. It was brazen and absolutely wanton—and so completely alien to anything Liza had ever done. But she wanted it. She wanted to lose herself in the fire of Jacob's mouth, hands and eager body.

Jacob deposited her on the couch just long enough to pause and remove his own shirt, then he lay down beside her. Tenderly he brushed a strand of gold from her flushed forehead. "I'll make it so good for you, Liza—the best you've ever known."

She wanted to tell him then, wanted him to know this was the first time. There had been no other time, no other man before this. But somehow it didn't matter now. For even if she had known other men as intimately, as fully, as utterly completely as Liza was about to know Jacob, it would be as if he were a pi-

oneer, blazing new trails of fulfillment within her
aching soul. She thirsted toward him like a flower
opening its petals to the falling rain, and Jacob
clasped her bare hips, pressing his hot, eager mouth
against the smooth skin of her thigh. Liza could only
reach out and caress the muscled hardness of his naked shoulders. She had never seen him without a
shirt and was astonished at how powerfully the man
was built.

How was it possible? she asked herself with awe.
After years of holding back, after all the doubts and
recriminations, how had it happened so quickly?
Was this part of the magic of love? She had fought
and refused to yield until the wedding night, yet she
had known Jacob Van Cleef less than a single week.
There was something so right, so natural, so completely fitting about this lovemaking. She had known
Jacob for a handful of days, yet she had known him
forever. Liza had been waiting for this man, for this
ultimate moment since she knew enough to wish for
love. And then, effortlessly, the words came. They
flowed up from Liza's heart and onto her lips without any fear of shyness.

"I love you," Liza whispered.

Jacob stiffened. "You *what*?"

"I love you, Jacob!" It was so delicious to tell
him. To finally say the words.

He pulled himself up sharply and stared down at
her. "Say that again!"

"I love—"

He put a finger to her lips. "It's all right, Liza," came out the rasp. "You don't have to go overboard."

"I don't understand," she gazed up at him in bewilderment.

"I know you like me, and I know we're about to go to bed together, but you don't have to overdo it, honey." There was a layer of cynical amusement to his words. "You don't have to sugarcoat it for me."

"What are you talking like this for?" Liza was appalled. "I tell you I love you, and you say not to overdo it?" She shook her head in disbelief and shock. "Why are you behaving this way?"

"Oh, don't act so outraged, Liza." His eyes narrowed. "I can enjoy a good joke as well as the next person."

"A joke?" she practically gasped. "You call this a *joke*?" Here she had just poured out her heart to the man, and he was calling it all a joke. This had to be a nightmare!

"Don't look so wounded, darling." He smiled soothingly. "Your performance was almost convincing."

"My *what*?" Liza practically choked. This was worse than any bad dream. This was a blackness darker than any despair she'd felt at Mark's betrayal. This was inconceivable. Insanity. Endless night.

"Don't you worry about anything, Liza. You've still won." He reached out to touch a naked breast with the total confidence of possession. "I'll give you everything you want. I can afford it, as you well know."

She felt a sickness in her stomach. "What do you mean, 'afford it?' Afford *what*?" Something unpleasant and dangerous hovered in the air between them.

"You don't have to play the outraged damsel any longer," Jacob remarked matter-of-factly. "I know very well what your game is, Liza."

"And what game is that?" The words were dragged from her lips.

"The money game, what else?"

"I must be very stupid," she said coldly. "You'll have to spell it out for me."

His gaze was frank and honest. "It's all right. I know you were looking for a rich husband, but I don't mind as long as we can be open about it."

"So," her jaw tightened, "that's what this is all about."

Jacob's finger drew a leisurely path to her other round breast, circling it with pleasure. "I'm willing to marry you, Liza. In fact, I think it's a pretty sensible idea."

"A rich husband," she breathed hollowly. "You think I'm that cheap, that mercenary?"

"Why is it so upsetting to hear the truth? If I don't mind, why should you?"

Liza shook her head numbly. "What happened to the man who told me all those wonderful things last night? I bare my heart to you, and you treat me like cheap gold digger!''

"I was crazy last night," he muttered. "I didn't know what I was saying. But I never lied. I've always wanted you, Liza, and that's the truth." Something strange was beginning to touch Jacob at the outer edges of his consciousness. It slipped beneath the edges to slowly pull away the layer of poison that had colored his vision. Why was she so upset? he wondered.

"You never even bothered to ask me to explain *why* I was so confused last night, did you?" Liza stared at him with flintlike eyes. "You never asked me why I seemed to be struggling with my own mixed feelings. When I begged you to give me time, you carried on like some macho lunatic!"

"You teased me last night," he insisted stubbornly.

"A lot you know about women, Mr. Jacob Van Cleef!" Liza wrenched free of his confining embrace and slid away from him on the leather couch. More furious than embarrassed, she grabbed her shirt and bra up from where they lay carelessly strewn on the floor.

Jacob watched her begin to dress with hooded eyes. "You played a game with me last night. Do you deny it?"

"Of course I deny it, and as long as we're on the subject of games—" Liza finished snapping closed the front hook of her bra and pulled her T-shirt angrily over her tousled blond head "—just who the hell do you think *you* are, toying with my feelings the way you did?"

"I haven't toyed with you, Liza. I've been honest and open about everything." He still didn't understand, and yet for the first time since Liza had walked into his office, Jacob began to see a young woman who was hurt and angry. The reality of what she seemed to be trying to tell him was so unlikely, so remote a possibility, that it staggered him to consider it.

"Oh, shut up and listen to me, you overgrown phony!" Liza couldn't believe the fury in her voice. She was a tornado of anger now, and nothing was going to stand in the path of her rage. "I asked you to be patient with me, and you go on a mad tirade!"

Jacob stood in stunned fascination, growing more and more apprehensive by the minute.

"It never occurred to you—" Liza pulled up her denims and tucked the tails of her shirt forcefully into the waistband "—it never even *occurred* to you, did it, that I might be afraid of an intimacy with any man? That I might not be as experienced as you apparently think I am?"

"What are you talking about?"

"Oh, so now you're listening, are you?" Her voice was remote, bitter. "Let's leave my inexperience out of this for a moment. It also never occurred to you that I might possibly be afraid of my feelings? Maybe I was getting over a broken heart and needed time to heal, and that was my reason for escaping from Washington.''

"Is that true?" he asked metallically.

"Don't you remember asking who had hurt me?"

"Yes, and you denied it." His voice was accusing now.

"Maybe I wasn't ready to talk about it." She shrugged. "It happened less than two weeks ago."

"What happened?" A vein in his neck throbbed. "What happened two weeks ago, Liza?"

She looked at him levelly. "I broke my engagement."

"You were engaged . . . to another man? Who the hell was he?"

"That's not important."

"It sure as hell is!" he boomed. "Why did you break it off?"

"That's none of your business."

"It damn well *is* my business!"

"If you really insist on knowing, it was because he betrayed my trust."

"How?" came the hard interjection.

"With other women."

Jacob shot her a disbelieving glance. "You mean he had you but still wanted other women? What was he, nuts?"

In a perverse way, she found Jacob's outrage strangely gratifying. "It doesn't matter now."

"Why?"

"Because he doesn't exist any more."

And now, suddenly, the outer edges of Jacob's mind grasped the reality of what had been staring him in the face for so long. He began to see it with a dawning, crystal clarity that made him question his own sanity. "Tell me why he doesn't exist now," he uttered huskily.

"I already told you why. You weren't listening."

"Tell me—for God's sake, Liza!"

She shook her head bitterly. "You've gone too far today, Jacob."

"Tell me!" he demanded again, rising from the sofa.

"I'll never say those words again," came the sad response.

"You said you loved me." He started toward Liza and the light, happily grasping the truth at last. "You told me you were in love with me!" Jacob towered over her, barely inches away now.

She turned her head from his heated gaze. "I loved you when I walked into the room, Jacob, I admit it. But that was before. I'll never forget what you accused me of." She headed toward the door.

"Liza, wait!" He wore a look of such pain and self-loathing, that she almost went back into his arms. "How can I explain to you—"

Liza stopped him with a wave of her hand. "No, Jacob. I don't want to hear it. Not now." She lowered her moistened eyelashes to gaze unseeing at the carpet. "Before, when it would have meant something . . . I would have listened. I would have listened to anything you wanted to tell me.''

Jacob stood there, still dumbstruck, paralyzed. Lunatic! bonehead! he remonstrated himself savagely. What the hell was his problem? How could he have thrown away such a sweet gift, offered to him so openly, so freely? Liza had told him of her love and he'd not merely mocked her—he had been unspeakably cruel. Was this what the years had done to him? Was this irrational, blind moron actually himself? "Liza, please—" he began, only to be stopped cold by the look in her silver-blue eyes.

"Forget it, Jacob. I'm leaving." Her hand reached for the doorknob and unfastened the lock.

Jacob stared at her wildly, in desperation. He knew he could go to Liza right now and bodily prevent her from leaving his office. She was small and slender. It would take no effort at all to lift her off the floor and carry her back to the couch in the corner. There he could effectively smother all her angry protests with kisses—kisses so urgent and persuasive that they would convince her of his need to be forgiven. "Liza," he tried again.

She was beyond listening to him now. "Don't say anything more." Her expression wasn't even angry; it was merely dull and listless. Broken.

"If you'd just give me a chance—" This time he was the one who begged, but it didn't matter. Jacob knew any action would be futile. He had never felt so utterly helpless, so completely ineffectual.

Liza opened the door to the office and walked away without another word, leaving a stricken Jacob Van Cleef behind her.

# Chapter Nine

Liza flatly refused to discuss anything about what had happened between her and Jacob with Tracy, so her friend was forced to come to her own conclusions. She told Liza she'd seen Jake wandering around the village on his usual errands and couldn't help but notice the circles under his eyes and the pallor and strain that even a tan could not conceal. In fact, Tracy had told Liza, he looked so woebegone and lost that Tracy actually forgot how much she was supposed to dislike the man and felt sorry for him instead. The occasions that he came by to visit the twins, she could see the tension in his face as he searched for any sign of Liza, her friend reported. But Liza was steadfastly avoiding him. As soon as she heard his truck pulling into the driveway she went directly up to the attic bedroom and remained there until he left again.

Liza knew Tracy must be baffled about why Liza had decided to hang around—because Liza was wondering the same thing herself. But as the days passed she began to understand. She might be confused and unhappy about Jacob Van Cleef, but returning to Washington was no solution. She had little doubt what would await her there upon her return. On the other hand, she had actually come to care for this enchanted hamlet. It was tranquil and soothing, with the exception of her debacle with Jacob.

But why stay, Liza wondered, with the pain so fresh? Then at last she realized the truth. Unlike the humiliating finality of Mark's betrayal, there was still unfinished business with Jacob. As deep as the hurt from his odd behavior was, she knew that she still loved him. Mark had truly rejected Liza, but Jacob's error had been one of misjudgment. He was so hardened by his past experiences that he simply had been unable to accept the reality of Liza's feelings for him.

Slowly, Liza began to grasp the difference between the superficial affection she'd felt for Mark Sheridan and true love: the superficial kind could not withstand hurt, but genuine love was far more resilient. It could absorb the blows inflicted so carelessly upon it and learn to heal itself from within. She had not stopped loving Jacob overnight. Those ties still linked her to him inexorably. It might be painful, far too painful to see him or speak to him right now, but it would have been even more unbearable to be away from him completely.

She was a realist, after all, Liza thought—her father's daughter. Hadn't she been told that often enough? She felt her lips twist cynically. Realistically, she accepted human nature and its weaknesses. The truth of the matter was that despite resistance, insults and rejection, human beings would always fight for the things they believed in.

Deep down inside, Liza realized, she still believed in Jacob. Eventually, she would be unable to resist falling under his spell again. One day, she might even open her wounded heart to him again. By then he might be ready to accept her love. Maybe time would teach him to learn to trust. Liza sighed heavily. On the other hand, it was still a profound risk. For if, even with the passage of time, Jacob still hesitated to accept the gift of her heart, there was nothing left to be done.

Late Friday night Tracy came home full of news of a major crisis at the Fralinglitch Inn. A bout of the summer flu had sidelined much of the staff, including the banquet manager.

"They're going bananas," Tracy declared. "They've got three major events scheduled in the next week, and there's no time to cancel." She stared at Liza with a speculative air.

"Okay, what's up?"

"What do you mean?" Tracy looked innocent.

"When you get that intense look, I know you're cooking up something."

"Well, it's just that it's such a jam they're in. I happened to mention my friend, who's an ex-banquet manager... and hey! What a coincidence, she just happens to be here for a visit!"

"I have no experience in the restaurant business—"

"Oh, c'mon! Haven't you organized sit-down dinners for eight hundred people, not to mention fund-raisers, benefits and at least one party of the century?"

"But I know nothing about the Fralinglitch Inn, its cuisine, the facilities...."

"What's to know? A restaurant is a restaurant and you've been to 'em all. Besides, what they really need is someone in charge to delegate responsibility and make sure everything runs smoothly. Just your cup of tea."

"Trace—"

"Listen, Liza, I wouldn't be asking unless we were really stuck. Besides we'd be able to hang out together, just like old times."

In the end Liza agreed. She told herself it was as a favor to Tracy and her co-workers, but the truth was she needed to be busy again. The lack of diverting activity was threatening to calcify her brain.

* * *

It had been called by many names over the years, including The Devil's Horseshoe, The Blue Coach and Three Chimneys, but the pre-Revolutionary building on the outskirts of town would always be known by its geographic designation, The Fralinglitch Inn. A colonial-style country inn with a pleasing blend of authentic and reproduced early American furniture, the inn boasted three huge brick fireplaces that formed the focal point of the rustic decor. In the summer months the fireplaces were filled with blooming plants, Liza noted as she looked appreciatively around the welcoming building.

Tracy's word was apparently worth a great deal to the other staff members, because Liza was hired and accepted without discussion or argument. The three events she was to help run were two weddings and a local fund-raiser for the county sheriff. Once Liza became familiar with the kitchens and the food staff, everything else was a snap. As far as the wedding receptions were concerned, she knew all about running the perfect affair—from where to place the flowers to how to create imaginative table settings. The food had been ordered in advance by the families of the wedding couples, and Liza made sure about when and how quickly to serve each course. Compared to the large, unwieldy affairs she was used to organizing, her work at the Fralinglitch was duck soup. The last assignment that week was to plan and execute the county sheriff gala, featuring the basic prime rib and potato meal that old-time politicians adored.

The afternoon of the dinner Liza, dressed in her pink silk blouse and skirt, which had become her work "uniform," was sitting in the office of the banquet manager, writing down some last-minute notes. Liza smiled as she wrote, more than satisfied with the work she'd been doing. The two brides had been delighted with her supervision of their weddings; the staff—from the busboys to the maître d'— considered her a godsend; and it was wonderful to be able to talk to Tracy. With her bubbly personality and infinite patience, Tracy was the most popular waitress at the inn. Nevertheless, it was a waste that Tracy was forced to stay here, instead of pursuing her career prospects.

Liza didn't even hear him come in. Jacob was just *there* all of a sudden, standing silently next to her desk. This time he was waiting for *her* to look up from a paper.

Finally he said, "Are you ever going to forgive me?"

It was then that she looked up. He had lost weight in the past week, and there were new hollows in his cheeks. The lines near his eyes made him look more gaunt than ever. He was dressed in an immaculate gray suit with a deep charcoal tie. He appeared weary and wonderful at the same time. "Hello, Jacob," Liza began slowly. "What brings you here?"

"I'll be giving the introductory speech for Sheriff Fenner tonight, and—"

"Really?" she interrupted bitingly. "I had no idea you took such an active interest in local politics."

He sighed. "I know the last person you want to see right now is standing here feeling like the major jerk of all time—" his voice was pained "—but this is business."

Liza was strangely disappointed. "Business?"

Stiffly Jacob removed a memo pad from inside his well-cut jacket. "There are going to be some important people here tonight, and it's crucial not to step on any of their sensitive egos. I'd like to double-check with you concerning the seating arrangements."

"Of course," she replied, deflated. "By all means let's review this crucial situation. We'd certainly not want to bruise any delicate egos and ruin your little fund-raiser for the sheriff of Nottingham."

"Sheriff Fenner," he corrected wearily, "and I deserved that. I deserve everything you're saying to me, and even the things I know you're thinking right now."

Liza could see the pain and regret so achingly evident in his expression. "There you go again," she whispered softly, "claiming to know what's on my mind."

He raised a hopeful eyebrow. "Am I right for once?"

Suddenly, it was too much to even look at him. Liza forced her eyes down on her desk, staring at a page of cost figures that began to blur into each other. "You said you were here on business—"

"Damn it, Liza!" he said in frustration, "when are you ever going to learn to read *my* mind!" He angrily tossed the memo pad to the ground. "Why the hell would I care where a bunch of ridiculous place cards go? Who gives a rap about sensitive little egos and where they sit?"

"This is interesting. Go on." She studied him with incredible calm.

"I needed an excuse, all right?" He leaned over the desk heavily. "For days I've been wracking my brains, trying to figure out some way to approach you."

"All right," she said with a shrug, "so you found a way."

"Now that I've approached you," Jacob continued unsteadily, "here comes the hard part."

Liza swallowed. "Oh, and what part is that?" The ballpoint pen she clutched so tightly stabbed repeatedly into the desk blotter as she spoke.

"Approaching you was relatively easy. Getting you to listen is something else." Jacob gazed down at her, his brown eyes dull and sad. "I can't even get you to look at me."

There was a long silence. Slowly Liza raised her head and met his pained stare. "All right, Jacob. I'm listening."

"Then I'll repeat what I said when I first walked in here. Are you ever going to forgive me?" He was waiting, strangely vulnerable. "Please, Liza, answer me."

She swallowed, already knowing the answer, but unsure how to cast aside the last remaining traces of pride and hurt. "Jacob, I—" Liza began.

"Please, Liza." The man was practically begging. "I was an idiot. Won't you ever accept my apology and let me have a second chance?"

But Liza knew what she was waiting for, and until she heard it, there was no point in uttering the response she yearned to give. The response that would set them both free.

Jacob's jaw tightened. "A week ago, you came into my office and said you loved me." There was a pause. "Now it's *my* turn."

Liza's heart leapt, but she dared not acknowledge the dream. "Your turn for what?"

"Because if you give me a second chance, I'll do all the things I should have done the first time, honey."

"Your turn for *what*?" she repeated calmly.

He exhaled raggedly. "To tell you that I love you. I love you, Liza, do you hear me?"

The warm glow of joy exploded through the essence of everything that was Liza, past and present. It obliterated the last dark vestiges of doubt with the blinding incandescence of a million lights. "I hear you, Jacob," she answered.

There was a hopeful hesitation, but Jacob still seemed unsure. "And?" he demanded. "Are you saying that it's all right, and you forgive me?"

"I forgive you."

"But do you still love me, Liza?"

"This is a pretty poor showing," she uttered softly, "for a man who claims to be a mind reader. In fact, I would strongly suggest pursuing another line of work if you wish to continue your career in a carnival. How about becoming a magician?"

"Liza," he said, his voice strained, "are you going to answer me or not? Lord knows, I deserve to be tortured like this, but enough is enough! Do you still care, or have I managed to kill any feelings you ever had for me?"

Liza couldn't bear to inflict any more pain on him. She had never meant to punish Jacob, never meant to make him suffer for even an instant. "Of course I still care," she whispered. "I never stopped loving you, Jacob. Couldn't you tell?"

"God!" he marveled, "you still love me?" In a moment he was around the desk, pulling her up from the swivel chair and into his arms. His dark eyes glittered with a happiness that had never before revealed such joy in their depths. "I can't believe how lucky I am!" Jacob cupped her face with his strong but gentle fingers. "Oh, Liza," he shook his head wonderingly, "how can you manage to love the world's stupidest human being?"

"It hasn't been easy," she murmured beneath her breath with a joking smile. She wrapped her arms around his waist. How delicious it was to have him this way—so accessible, so open to her love at last...all barriers torn down. "I was wondering how long it was going to take you to find out where I worked."

He was incredulous. "Wait a minute. Are you saying that you've been waiting all this time—"

Liza stared back at him teasingly. "Yes."

"You mean, all I had to do was walk in here, and you would have been mine again?"

"That's about the size of it, Jacob." She was surprised how easily the words came now.

He hesitated, "You do accept the fact that you're mine, and you belong only to *me*, don't you Liza?"

She smiled. Sure, she was still her own person, and Jacob was still his own person, but the fact was it worked both ways. He was *hers* now, also. Yet, within the bonds that tied their love together they were still individuals who would always be free to express their needs and dreams. It might seem contradictory, but that was the complex and beautiful nature of love, Liza realized. "Yes, I do," she conceded with happiness, not from weakness but from strength, and gave herself up to his heated embrace.

This time his kisses were unbelievably tender, with a gentleness and reverence he had never used before.

"I never thought it was possible to feel this way about anyone," Jacob murmured against her hair.

"Oh, Jake," she breathed, "I wish we didn't have this banquet tonight!"

"Why not?" he asked between urgent nibbles along the sensitive cord of her neck.

"I just want to be alone with you."

"How alone do you mean, honey?" His eyes held an alien glint.

"You know what I mean," she trembled, almost too shy to tell him what she needed.

"Are you saying that you want me to make love to you?"

"Yes," she nodded.

He uttered a hoarse sound of joy. "Tonight, Liza, I intend to take you home with me and love you until you cry out for mercy!"

"Oh, Jake!"

He pulled her more tightly against his male hardness, the frank arousal evident even now. Once again his lips claimed her mouth, tasting and exploring the trembling moistness. Liza clung to him, thigh to thigh, her breasts straining through the thin silk of her blouse against the rough texture of his jacket. Mindless with the strength of her feelings, she ground her hips into his lean, taut body, inciting Jacob into a more and more intimate caress. But soon it was Jacob himself who pulled away with an agonized groan.

"If I don't stop now, Liza, I won't be able to." He looked down at her flushed face, swollen lips and bright eyes. "Somehow, I already know what you'll look like when we actually make love—" he paused thickly "—*tonight*."

# Chapter Ten

In the best of all possible worlds all things run smoothly, like the inner workings of a well-oiled machine. And at first Liza thought that was how things were finally going for her. The man she loved would be taking her home with him that evening, following a successful fund-raiser for the reelection of Mr. Otis T. Fenner for county sheriff. Everyone would continue to congratulate the newest visitor to Half Moon Falls for her wonderful organizational skills in catering. On top of that, the day would come when she would, at last, reconcile Tracy and Jacob.

*In the best of all possible worlds.*

"I'm happy for you, I truly am," said Tracy.

The two of them were relaxing in Liza's office half an hour after Jacob's visit, during Tracy's break. But Liza knew her friend too well. There was a heaviness to Tracy's words. "What is it? Are you uncomfortable with the idea of my marrying Jacob?"

"I can't tell you a lie, Liz. It doesn't thrill me, but—" she gave a helpless shrug "—I know he'll probably make you very happy. So what the heck, right?"

"I'm sorry for the way he hurt you and Peter."

"So am I."

"But I love him, Trace." Liza sighed. "What can I do?" Part of Liza was deliriously happy, but her conscience was still clouded by the torn loyalty.

"I know. Forget it, Liza," Tracy said, her tone philosophical. "Love's hard enough to find, without thinking you can actually choose the person. You couldn't help falling in love with the guy. It happens that way."

"But listen," Liza told her friend now, "I understand how you feel about Jacob. If I told you how tormented he is about having broken you and Peter up, would it help at all?"

"No." Tracy sighed again. "Now, Liz, I'm not going to be a pain about this, believe me. I'll come to your wedding—I'll even be bridesmaid if you want me to. I'll come to your house for Sunday dinner. But I'm sorry. Even though I intend to be cordial to the man who will be your husband, I can never feel anything for him except dislike.''

"But listen to me—''

"Don't try to change my mind. It's the way I feel, and you've got to let me live with it.''

"I wish things could be different.''

"So do I, but sometimes, when a wound goes too deep and a hurt is so great, it can never heal.''

"Then perhaps it's about time it did.'' Jacob stood in the doorway, his height towering above the two of them, a thoughtful, sad shadow.

Tracy's lips tightened. "I understand congratulations are in order.''

"This has gone on long enough.'' Jacob regarded Tracy's cold glance. "And it's wrong.''

"I know what you want to say, and forget it,'' Tracy dismissed the entreaty. "I'll never discuss it, ever.''

"But you don't know, Tracy.'' Jacob shook his head heavily. "You haven't the vaguest conception what I want to say.'' He spoke in tones so even, so controlled that both women were compelled to pay attention. "I thought that the end would justify the means. I thought it didn't matter how you felt about me as long as I did the right thing.''

"What 'right thing?''' Tracy's voice was hard. "You call breaking a girl's heart 'the right thing?'''

"Tracy," Jacob said, his voice actually quavering, "I had to break your heart. It was the only way to save your sanity."

There was a silence. "What are you talking about?"

"I've kept silent all these years because I thought anything would be better than you finding out the truth. Even your hatred seemed a price worth paying...."

Liza watched the scene unfold mutely. She felt as if she were the audience in a drama, helpless to do anything but watch the performance run its course.

"What truth?" Tracy barely whispered.

Jacob was strained. "How the hell can I tell you this, Tracy?"

"Tell me *what*? Please, Jake, what is it? How bad can it be?" Her words were a plea.

"When my father died, seven years ago, he told me—" Jacob raked his fingers through his hair in a harsh gesture "—that the woman who was living in town as his mistress had known him long *before* moving to Half Moon Falls." He looked at Tracy significantly. "Do you understand me? I said *before* she moved to town."

Tracy might have fallen backward if Liza hadn't reached out a supportive arm. "What are you trying to tell me, Jake?" Tracy asked shakily.

"Tracy," he uttered painfully, "I was executor of my father's estate. I found the letters in his safe from your mother. It proved what my father confessed to me the night he died."

"Jake," Tracy choked, "for God's sake, tell me!"

He shut his eyes for a moment. "He was your father. He was your father, Tracy, and all the time he knew."

"Oh, God." Tracy looked as if she were about to be sick.

"Do you see now," Jacob declared softly, "why I had to break you and Peter up? Heaven help me, it was the most difficult thing I've ever had to do."

Tracy sank numbly into the armchair. "All along, my mother knew that man was my father. And you and Peter—" She covered her mouth. "Do you have any idea what we almost—"

Quickly Jacob strode across the room and knelt beside her. "But it didn't happen, Tracy. And it's over. Forget it now."

Slowly, Tracy focused her attention on the man who was crouched next to her in concern. "All this time you let me believe...let me hate you—"

"Forget it," he replied brusquely. "It doesn't matter."

"Why didn't you tell me before?" She shook her head in disbelief.

"How could I? How could I expect you to deal with something like that?" He shrugged. "And the boys—"

"Jacob," Tracy asked, "is it true? Are we all—"

He touched his sister's shoulder comfortingly. "That's the strange part, Tracy. I'm sure about you being related, but I've never been one-hundred-percent positive about the twins. It's a pretty good guess, though, I'd say. They've certainly got the Van Cleef stubborn streak." It was an attempt at levity that seemed to be a little effective. It actually succeeded in eliciting a tiny laugh from Tracy.

Liza shook her head in wonderment. In just a few moments her friend's world had been transformed forever. When Tracy finally got over the shock Liza was confident that the unexpected discovery would soon be accepted. Tracy would learn to accept the past and welcome a new kind of future. A future complete with an unexpected heritage. Right now, she thought tactfully, the best possible thing to be done was to leave the office for a few moments and give the newfound siblings a chance to meet each other all over again.

Jacob's stunning revelation only served to make him even more of a marvel in Liza's eyes. It was a relief to know he had never been intentionally cruel to Tracy. Everything he had ever done had been for a reason. His willingness to allow his half sister to believe the worst of him showed Jacob's total lack of selfishness. He had lived with Tracy's undeserved hatred all these years, silently accepting it. It was an unexpected blessing, thought Liza. The seemingly irreparable rift at last was healed. She, Jacob, Tracy and the twins were one happy, united family. Everything was working out magnificently.

The sheriff's dinner began and ran smoothly enough. Otis Fenner, a fat, balding man with a congenial smile and soft voice was introduced at the podium by an unusually beaming Jacob Van Cleef. He gave the typical speech that Liza had heard at hundreds of these kinds of affairs, about keeping progress in step with the economy yet retaining old traditional values in a changing world. Liza smiled to herself as she stood by the door supervising the coffee service. Some things certainly remained the same in this world! It was then that she noticed the woman sitting next to Otis on the dais. She was a splendid figure in sleek black and pearls, her ash-colored hair swathed fashionably around her head in the perfect chignon. It couldn't be! It might be a changing world, Liza thought desperately, but surely it couldn't be such an incredibly *small* one.

And suddenly, from up on the dais, the elegant vision with the silver hair gave a shriek that might have awakened the dead. In Idaho. "I don't believe it! Elizabeth! Elizabeth, darling!"

Heads turned. Busboys stopped refilling water glasses. Tracy stopped dead in her tracks with the instincts of a combat veteran. If only Otis had not just finished his speech. If only the enthusiastic applause had not just died down. If only no one had heard the silver-haired woman's exclamation and followed the pointing of one long, red fingernail. It pointed directly at Liza.

Liza was filled with a sensation of impending doom that reminded her of the blockbuster adventure movie in which a giant boulder came hurtling down the passageway of a booby-trapped cave about to crush the hero beneath its deadly weight. "Damn," Liza muttered, half aloud.

"Otis, you'll never guess who *this* is!" The lady leaned forward over the table. Her name was Myra Jorgenson, and she was the widow of a U.S. congressman. Elizabeth had seen her at all the galas that she and her mother had ever been associated with. Myra was sixty years old if she was a day, and she was the worst gossip that anyone in Washington and its environs had ever had the misfortune to know.

"You'll never—oh, I can't imagine! Elizabeth Langley, what are you doing here, in Fralinglitch, of all places?"

"Langley?" repeated Jacob, who until now had been sitting on the dais on the other side of Otis, watching the entire scene unfold first with curiosity then with utter disbelief.

"You should be honored, Otis, absolutely! Arthur Langley's own little Elizabeth showing up to hear you speak... why that's practically an endorsement from the man, himself!"

"*Arthur* Langley!" Jacob practically choked.

"I do suspect, though, that she's slumming," Myra Jorgenson went on, gushing and rambling alternately. No one seemed to care that the microphones were still turned on.

"Well, how do you do, Miss Langley." Otis Fenner extended a meaty hand. "I'm a great admirer of your father. Why, I consider him to be one of the giants, keeping the world safe for democracy and our American way of life!"

*Oh, please!* Liza thought she was going to be ill. *This wasn't really happening. It had to be some bizarre hallucination!*

Jacob stared at Liza in utter shock. "You're Arthur Langley's daughter?"

Liza looked at him helplessly. What could she say? Nearby, Tracy gave her a sympathetic nod. All Liza could do now was take a deep breath and face the music. Slowly she walked toward the dais.

"So, how have you been, Mrs. Jorgenson?" Liza reluctantly extended her hand.

"How many times have I begged you to call me Myra?" the woman clucked. "You naughty girl, running off like that without a word to anyone. Not that I can blame you, with that dreadful Mark Sheridan and his peccadilloes! And him a United States senator! The man should be taken out and horsewhipped, my dear! Tarred and feathered! Washed and hung out to dry!"

Liza was praying for a hole to open up and swallow not herself, but Mrs. Myra Jorgenson.

Jacob had risen from his seat and walked slowly down toward her. His face was cold and unforgiving. "I don't believe we've met," he said, extending a rigid hand. "How do you do, Miss *Langley*."

"Please, Jacob," Liza pleaded beneath her breath, "don't be angry."

"Angry? Why should I be angry?" The tautness of his jaw told another story.

"I couldn't tell you who I was. I couldn't tell anyone!"

"Why?" came the clipped reply. "Was someone holding a gun to your head?"

"I needed to get away, where nobody knew me."

"When were you intending to tell me?"

"It just didn't seem very important at the time." Liza struggled to make him understand, not caring that the entire drama was unfolding before the two hundred guests of Otis Fenner and his campaign committee.

"What on earth is going on?" interjected Myra Jorgenson, her eyes bright with conjecture.

"You still haven't answered my question, Liza," grated out Jacob. "Exactly when were you going to tell me who you really were?"

"Jacob, you have to understand—"

"Oh, I understand plenty. Perhaps you never intended to tell me at all."

"You don't mean that!"

"Sure," he continued roughly. "What was the word our dear friend Myra just used—*slumming?* Was that what you were doing, Liza? Just slumming?"

"What a dreadful thing to say!" Two bright spots of pink suffused her face.

"Were you intending to have your little diversion with some hick farmer in the boondocks, and then when you got bored return to dear Daddy and the mansion and parties?"

"Of course not!" she denied hotly.

His eyes were two narrow slits. "You don't mean to tell me that it wasn't a comedown?"

"What are you talking about?"

"From U.S. senator to yokel dairyman!"

"How can you compare yourself to Mark Sheridan?" she cried.

"I can't. That's the problem, isn't it?"

Now she understood his hurt and anger. He was afraid she couldn't love him the way she was supposed to care for her tabloid prince. "I meant that you're so far superior to him in every way that there's absolutely no contest. Don't you see?"

"Liza!" he practically growled, "the man is rich, handsome—"

"*You're* rich and handsome," she challenged.

"Not the way he is."

"That's a matter of opinion."

"No, it's a matter of fact," came the sad reply. "Not to mention the fact that he might very well be president of the United States one day."

"Not likely, after *that* scandal, I can tell you!" declared Myra.

"I beg your pardon, Mrs. Jorgenson—" Liza began sharply.

"Myra."

"But would you very much mind," Liza continued, "staying the heck out of this?"

"I'm only trying to help clarify things," the woman sniffed, greatly offended.

"Nobody asked you, Myra!" Jacob took his shot at the meddling socialite, then returned to the matters at hand. "You expect me to believe that the idea of being the First Lady doesn't send shivers of excitement right up your blue-blooded spine?" His tone had never been so caustic.

"Only if she reconciles with Mark," reasoned Myra. "All could be forgiven, on the other hand, and one never can tell how the political tide could—"

"Butt out!" Liza cried in utter frustration. "Can't you see this is a personal matter between me and my fiancé?"

"Fiancé?" Jacob rasped, "You mean to tell me that you actually intend to—"

"Oh, are you going back on your proposal?" she inquired tartly.

"I never thought you—"

"Oh, you hoped I misunderstood, did you?"

"Fiancé!" Myra Jorgenson exclaimed in amazement. "Liza, my dear, however do you manage to pick up the slack so quickly?"

"Please shut up, Myra!" begged Otis.

Jacob stared ominously at Liza. "Let me get this straight. You're saying that you *want* to marry me?"

"Darn right, I do. And by the way, so did you, just this afternoon. Or have you forgotten so quickly?"

He shook his head in disbelief. "I haven't forgotten at all."

"You'd better not," Liza retorted loftily, "or I'll slap you with a breach of promise suit so fast you won't ever know what hit you."

"Tell him, Liz!" Tracy called out from the crowd.

"You'd sue me, hmm?" A faint smile began to soften Jacob's harsh features. "Is that a fact?"

"That's a fact."

"Is Jacob Van Cleef your fiancé or not?" one of the busboys shouted.

"He'd better be," Liza remarked blandly, "considering he tried to seduce me in his office just a few days ago."

"He did what?" interjected the maître d'.

"For crying out loud!" Jacob groaned. "This is a small town, Liza!"

"I still haven't heard you announce our engagement," she retorted, her eyes sparkling with a promise of more mischief.

"Is it what you really want?" Jake's brown eyes glimmered strangely. "Are you absolutely sure, honey?"

"Absolutely," she whispered. "Are you?"

"I've always been sure, Liza. Ever since that first day when you stood in the middle of the road, yelling your head off at me." He looked at Otis Fenner. "With your indulgence, Sheriff, I'd like to make a brief statement."

"Be my guest." The plump man waved his hand with a grin.

"Everyone—" Jacob put his arms around Liza tenderly "—I would like to introduce you all to the future Mrs. Van Cleef." There was a strange mist in Jacob's eyes as cheers and applause broke out in the banquet room.

As might have been expected, it took a while for the general hubbub to die down. Most of the buzz in the Fralinglitch Inn had little to do with the once and future sheriff of the county but concerned instead the incredibly romantic pas de deux that had unfolded right before hundreds of eyes. The stormy courtship of the famous Elizabeth Langley and the most eligible bachelor within a radius of thirty miles was a sensation.

"You'd have to go to the movies to see excitement like that," declared Tiny Baylor, the bartender, within Liza's hearing.

It promised to be a major topic of juicy discussion for months to come—Half Moon Falls had gotten itself the village's first honest-to-goodness celebrity.

"Not just a celebrity, but a celebrity *romance*!" gushed the social events editor of *The Fralinglitch Gazette* to a beaming Liza. "This is even better than Charles and Diana. A society princess, daughter of one of the most renowned statesmen of the century, giving up the hand of a future president to marry a local farmer!"

"I don't think we're ever going to live this down, honey," Jacob remarked embarrassedly when they were finally able to escape the eager crowd. "Everywhere you go in Half Moon Falls people are going to point and smile." He was guiding her down the curving path to the falls. The stars had already begun to come out.

"I won't mind that at all, not here," Liza answered, smiling back at him. She stumbled happily against him the rest of the way until the two of them stood at the base of the waterfall, where it emptied into the pond. So this was the magic of the falls at night, she marveled. The moon glimmered its white reflection in the deep black water. It truly was enchantment.

Jacob pulled her tight against him. "Of course you know they'll all be pointing because they'll wish they were in my place," he said gruffly, burying his lips against her ear. "Liza, you've brought me everything I could have possibly imagined."

And later when Jacob took her home, they brought each other still more than either could ever have imagined.

*   *   *   *   *

*Silhouette Intimate Moments*

# At Dodd Memorial Hospital, Love is the Best Medicine

When temperatures are rising and pulses are racing, Dodd Memorial Hospital is the place to be. Every doctor, nurse and patient is a heart specialist, and their favorite prescription is a little romance. Next month, finish Lucy Hamilton's Dodd Memorial Hospital Trilogy with HEARTBEATS, IM #245.

Nurse Vanessa Rice thought police sergeant Clay Williams was the most annoying man she knew. Then he showed up at Dodd Memorial with a gunshot wound, and the least she could do was be friends with him—if he'd let her. But Clay was interested in something more, and Vanessa didn't want that kind of commitment. She had a career that was important to her, and there was no room in her life for any man. But Clay was determined to show her that they could have a future together—and that there are times when the patient knows best.

---

*Silhouette Intimate Moments*

# MORE THAN A MIRACLE
## by Kathleen Eagle

This month, let award-winning author Kathleen Eagle sweep you away with a story that proves the truth of the old adage, "Love conquers all."

Elizabeth Donnelly loved her son so deeply that she was willing to sneak back to De Colores, an island paradise to the eye, but a horror to the soul. There, with the help of Sloan McQuade, she would find the child who had been stolen from her and carry him to safety. She would also find something else, something she never would have expected, because the man who could work miracles had one more up his sleeve: love.

Enjoy Elizabeth and Sloan's story this month in *More Than A Miracle*, Intimate Moments #242. And if you like this book, you might also enjoy *Candles in the Night* (Special Edition #437), the first of Kathleen Eagle's De Colores books.

---

# COMING NEXT MONTH

**#586 HEART OF GOLD—Sondra Stanford**
Melanie Jones, devoted manager of Ettinger's department store,
didn't have time for love, but Franklin Harrison Ettinger III was
determined to show her that woman does not live by career alone....

**#587 THE NEW KID IN TOWN—Stella Bagwell**
Widow Natalie Fuller loved coaching her son's Little League baseball
team, but her new coaching partner, rugged ex-cowboy Matt Tanner,
was more than distracting. Was Natalie falling for the new kid in town?

**#588 THE GIFT—Marie Ferrarella**
When Eve Tarrington and her kids appeared on Luke Randall's
doorstep in a snowstorm, he'd had to offer them shelter. Now he was
snowbound with Eve and her family—and the cabin was growing
unseasonably warm....

**#589 MURPHY'S LAW—Marcine Smith**
Farmer Thane MacDougal thought he needed a full-time homemaker
for his son, Murphy, but irresistible Meghan Forester—a dedicated
veterinarian—was going to shake up his straitlaced notions!

**#590 TRUCK DRIVING WOMAN—Elizabeth August**
Handsome, wealthy Cole York was way out of truck driver Darcy
Raines's league. He'd never be more to her than a self-appointed
guardian—or so she thought ... until he kissed her.

**#591 BY HOOK OR BY CROOK—Joan Smith**
Shawna Cassidy had become an amateur spy to catch mysterious Kurt
Slater stealing her uncle's designs. But by mistake she'd met
him ... and now he was stealing her heart!

---

### Silhouette Romance

# LONG, TALL TEXANS

## A Trilogy by Diana Palmer

Bestselling Diana Palmer has rustled up three rugged heroes in a trilogy sure to lasso your heart! The titles of the books are your introduction to these unforgettable men:

### CALHOUN

In June, meet Calhoun Ballenger. He wants to protect Abby Clark from the world, but can he protect her from himself?

### JUSTIN

Calhoun's brother, Justin—the strong, silent type—has a second chance with the woman of his dreams, Shelby Jacobs, in August.

### TYLER

October's long, tall Texan is Shelby's virile brother, Tyler, who teaches shy Nell Regan to trust her instincts—especially when they lead her into his arms!

Don't miss CALHOUN, JUSTIN and TYLER—three gripping new stories coming soon from Silhouette Romance!